LEVI

LIGHTHOUSE SECURITY INVESTIGATIONS

MARYANN JORDAN

Levi (Lighthouse Security Investigation) Copyright 2020

All rights reserved. No part of this book may be reproduced or transmitted in any form or by any means, electronic or mechanical, including photocopying, recording, or by any information storage and retrieval system without the written permission of the author, except where permitted by law.

If you are reading this book and did not purchase it, then you are reading an illegal pirated copy. If you would be concerned about working for no pay, then please respect the author's work! Make sure that you are only reading a copy that has been officially released by the author.

This book is a work of fiction. Names, characters, places, and incidents either are products of the author's imagination or are used fictitiously. Any resemblance to actual persons, living or dead, events, or locales is entirely coincidental.

Cover by: Graphics by Stacy

ISBN ebook: 978-1-947214-70-5

ISBN print: 978-1-947214-71-2

❀ Created with Vellum

1

"Hey, Levi. Bet you're ready to head out."

Levi Amory grinned as he shut the door to his SUV while holding the phone with his other hand. It was late in the evening, but he planned on an early start the next morning. "You've got that right, Tate. The SUV's tank is full, and the U-Haul is loaded." Frank Tate was a friend and soon-to-be coworker.

"So, you're still starting out in the morning?"

"Yeah, but don't expect me right away. I'm going to take a whole week to drive to Maine. I'll look like a fuckin' tourist, but that's what I'm going to be for a few days."

"Hell, after tours as a Ranger and agent with the FBI, you deserve a chance to be a tourist."

"That's what I thought. With no family in the area, since I landed in Wyoming, all I've done is work for the Bureau. I haven't had a vacation in years."

"Then you're definitely due. The rest of the guys are

looking forward to seeing you again, and we'll have the cabin ready for you when you get here."

"Give Nora my best, and I'll see you in a week." Disconnecting, he continued to grin as he walked into his rental condo. When he first became an agent stationed in Wyoming, he had no idea how long he might be there, so it didn't make sense to buy a house. He had found a condo at a reasonable rate, satisfied to rent. Now, as he stepped through the front door, it looked bare. *Not that I was ever into decorating anyway.*

The sofa and bed would be left behind, not wanting to haul them across the country. His personal belongings and smaller pieces of furniture fit into the U-Haul trailer attached to his SUV. Living out of boxes for the past week had gotten old, but now, standing in the almost empty condo, it looked strange. *Strange... yet good. It's time for a change.*

The refrigerator and cabinets were cleaned out, so there was no food left in the condo. But then, he also didn't have to worry about garbage to dispose of before leaving. Having eaten at a local diner for dinner, he planned to get breakfast on the road once he left in the morning.

With nothing left to do but not yet ready to go to bed, he settled onto the sofa, his mind turning to the many places he'd lived and said goodbye to. An Army brat, he'd spent the first eighteen years of his life in nine different houses, some on bases. He had attended four elementary schools, two middle schools, and two high schools. Packing up, moving, and saying goodbye had become second nature.

For some, it was a hard childhood, but Levi liked his own company. His mom used to say that he could go days without playing with other children and be perfectly happy. *Maybe that was just what I got used to... all the kids on the military bases were used to temporary friends.*

Once he joined the Army, his life was more barracks, more moves, more tours of duty. Becoming a Ranger gave him a sense of belonging, one that he discovered he loved. But years of special operations were hell on the body and the mind, and working as an agent for the FBI gave him the adventure he craved.

Wyoming had been an interesting place to land. Plains and prairies, rolling hills and mountains, pastures and ranches and farms. The people were nice, but he made few friends. He had thought the Bureau would provide the same camaraderie that he'd found in the Army Rangers but discovered that he worked more alone than with others.

Uttering a long sigh, he tilted his head back and closed his eyes, thoughts still moving through his mind. Tate had crossed his path months ago when Tate's former girlfriend was kidnapped by a drug-running survivalist and taken into the mountains. Providing assistance, he discovered Tate worked for a private security company—Lighthouse Security and Investigations, based out of Maine. Owned by Mace Hanson, a former Special Forces and CIA Special Operator, the company hired other former military special ops, now known to each other as Keepers. Intrigued, Levi had found out all he could about LSI from Tate before interviewing for a position as one of LSI's Keepers.

He'd flown to the East Coast for the final interview with Mace and was stunned at the operation and facilities. Taking missions all over the world, LSI provided security and investigations for both private and government contracts. But, most importantly, they worked as a team, and the call to belong to a group again was strong.

He looked out of the condo window toward the mountain range in the distance as the sunset painted the sky. Maine could not be more different from Wyoming. Thick, lush forests. Ocean waves crashing against the rocky coastlines. LSI was headquartered in a decommissioned lighthouse and adjoining house, extending deep inside reinforced caves below the ground at the edge of the ocean.

He had met the other Keepers, and the decision to leave the FBI was clear. Now, he was anxious to start on the over two-thousand-mile trip. Opening his eyes, he stared at the ceiling for a moment, pondering his upcoming career change and move. *Jesus, it'd be nice to find a place to settle. A place that I could call home. Maybe, just maybe, this will be it.*

The early morning drive passed with perfect weather, beautiful scenery, and virtually no traffic. Within three hours, Levi crossed into Nebraska, leaving Wyoming behind. He supposed some people would feel melancholic when leaving a place they'd lived and worked in, but Levi was ready. *"If a man listens closely, he can tell when it's time to make a new decision... plot a new course...*

have a new adventure. Then he knows it's right." His grandfather's often-spoken words came back to him, and Levi knew the decision to leave the Bureau and Wyoming was right.

When mapping out his journey, he'd decided to stick to the highway, considering he was pulling the trailer. Nebraska only had one major highway cutting through the middle, and when he first entered the state, the view was just like what he left in Wyoming. Eventually the mountains fell away, leaving rolling hills, scenic forests, and flat farmland. Other than stopping for gas and snacks, he pushed his way to North Platte before stopping for lunch.

Foregoing the typical fast food chains, he found a local diner. Stretching his body as he alighted from the SUV, he caught the tantalizing scents of home cooking and his stomach growled its impatience. Once seated, the friendly waitress spouted off the specials, and he eagerly agreed with her recommendation. When she returned with his plate piled high, he dove into the barbecue meatloaf, mashed potatoes, and green beans. Topping the meal off with iced tea and apple pie, he eyed his empty plate and hoped the large meal wouldn't make him sleepy for the afternoon drive.

"I saw you drive up with the U-Haul," the waitress said as she refilled his glass. "You moving in or out?"

"Heading east. This is my first real stop on the journey." As he handed her cash for his lunch—including a large tip—he asked, "I plan on checking out some of the Pony Express places. Got any recommendations?"

Eyes as bright as her smile, she nodded with enthusiasm. "There's the Gothenberg Station museum since you're heading east. It's got a nice little museum at the old station, but I warn you, it's not very big."

"Sounds like it's just my thing." With a nod and wave, he headed back outside. It didn't take long to get to the museum, and, true to her description, it was small but packed with Pony Express memorabilia, pictures, and information. Nearby was an old barn, and he pulled out his phone, snapping a few pictures, finding the weather-beaten structure fascinating considering it had stood the test of time.

Back on the road, he continued driving past Lincoln, having decided to spend the night at Ashland, home of the Strategic Air and Space Museum, a planned stop for the morning. As he pulled into the parking lot of the motel, he glanced at the odometer. A little over six hundred miles on the first leg of his journey. *Not a bad start for my first day.*

Making sure to secure the U-Haul and his SUV, he headed inside to register and get his key. The older gentlemen sitting behind the reception desk greeted him warmly.

"Just one night, and I need to be on the first floor where I can keep an eye on my vehicle."

"You're in luck 'cause it's a slow night. It'll be easy to put you where you want to be. Not much going on around here right now." He ran Levi's credit card before handing it back along with the room key. "We got us a little breakfast buffet, but I'll warn you, it's not real big. If you're going to be traveling tomorrow, you can't beat Mable's Pancake House just down the street. Not expensive, and she'll load you up with a good breakfast."

Tossing out his thanks and a smile, Levi headed to his room. Deciding to hit fast food for dinner, he walked two blocks and grabbed hamburgers, fries, and a milkshake. Once back in his room, he showered and lay on the bed. Television didn't appeal to him, but he dug out a book from his bag and read until his eyes grew heavy. The last thought he had before falling asleep was that so far, his trip was uneventful... just the way he wanted it. Easy. Uncomplicated.

Taking the advice of the receptionist, he had breakfast at Mable's and stared wide-eyed at his plate loaded with pancakes, scrambled eggs, and bacon. Looking around, he noticed the restaurant was mostly filled with couples, families, and gatherings of friends. It hit him that he was the only single person being served. Used to grabbing a meal while working, it had never caught his attention that he was generally alone. But here, in a popular restaurant located on a highway with many vacationers, it was glaringly evident.

Accepting the server's offer to take along a Pancake House travel mug of coffee, he settled behind the wheel and wondered if he was going to arrive in Maine ten pounds heavier than when he left Wyoming.

Once at the Air Command and Aerospace Museum, he wandered through the Korean War and Aviation exhibits. With interest, he moved into the Aircraft Collection, his footsteps echoing in the large, uncrowded building. He stopped at one of the restored airplanes, then slowly walked around the perimeter.

"It's a beauty, isn't it?"

Turning, he noticed an older man standing near him, and he offered a chin lift. "Yes, sir. My grandfather flew a B-29 Superfortress during the Korean War. I still have a picture of him standing in front of his plane."

The older man's bushy white eyebrows lifted to his forehead as he smiled widely. "No kidding?" He tapped his hand on his chest. "I'm a Korean War vet also, but I was in the Army. Came back and settled in this part of Nebraska. When I finally retired as a contractor, I told my wife that I'd go crazy sitting at home in a rocking chair, so I volunteer here."

Stepping closer, he shook the old man's hand. "My dad was also Army. So was I. From what I understand, my grandfather wanted my dad to become a pilot in the Air Force also, but he was determined to go his own way."

The older man cackled and nodded. "Oh, the young generally want to forge their own path." Cocking his head to the side, he said, "But you went into the Army like your dad."

"I suppose after being raised on Army bases all over the country, I couldn't think of anything else to do."

The two men continued to walk around, admiring the aircraft. "Here's another one from the Korean War. This one is the C-54 Skymaster. It was a passenger transport, probably not near as exciting as what your grandfather flew." He looked over at Levi and asked, "You just visiting?"

"Yes, sir. I'm changing jobs and changing scenery."

"You're still young. This is the perfect time to try

new things. I've loved my life, but I envy you. Sometimes, making a change is what keeps life exciting. Travel down a different road. It's all about finding new adventures."

With handshakes and goodbyes, Levi left the museum, thinking about the older man's words, so much like his grandfather's. *Exciting? Nah... I'd settle for simply interesting.*

His stomach rumbled, but he wanted to keep going. Opting for a drive through, he grabbed burgers and got back onto the highway. The mountains and rolling hills were left behind, and now the flat farmland of Iowa stretched out in front of him.

Used to being by himself, he listened to the radio for a little while then flipped over to an audiobook on military history that he had just begun before leaving Wyoming. Once again, the stories reminded him of the tales his grandfather used to tell and found himself wishing he still had the older man to talk to. His grandmother would occasionally roll her eyes when his grandfather began his war tales, but Levi had always found them fascinating.

He stopped occasionally in Iowa for gas and snacks while enjoying the non-crowded, leisurely drive. By dinner time he arrived at Davenport, Iowa, only slightly tired from the drive.

Having made reservations at a higher-end hotel right on the edge of the Mississippi River dividing Iowa and Illinois, he stepped into the modern-furnished room overlooking the river. Feeling the need for exercise, he changed into his swim trunks and headed to the hotel pool. The cool, refreshing water sluiced over his body, and the exercise stretched his muscles that were unused to spending hours in the car. Climbing out of the pool after an hour, he shook his head, slinging water to the sides, ignoring the gazes of two women in loungers, their eyes pinned on him.

Refreshed, his stomach growled, and he decided pizza delivered to his room would take care of his hunger. In the mood for a beer, he hit the hotel bar. As usual, it seemed that most people were paired together or in groups. Sitting at one end of the bar, he was nearly finished with his beer when a shadow fell across his drink. Glancing to the side, he saw a woman standing nearby.

"It should be a crime to have a man that looks like you sitting alone in a bar. But if you told me you were waiting on someone, it might break my heart."

Lifting his brow, he thought her line definitely showed a touch of creativity, if probably practiced. Her dress was just on the tad side of being a little too short and a little too tight. Her blood-red fingernails were long and filed to a point, forcing him to hide the shudder that moved through him. "I was just finishing and getting ready to leave," he said, hoping she would take the hint that he was not interested.

Unfortunately, it seemed to have the opposite effect. Her eyes widened and so did her smile. She attempted to link her arm through his as she leaned closer. "Perfect timing for me!"

Gently placing his hand over hers, he separated his arm from her claws and shook his head. "I'm afraid not.

Good night." With a slight incline of his head, he turned and walked out of the bar, her over-exaggerated huff meeting his ears.

Back in his room, he got ready for bed, but sleep did not come as readily. He thought about the woman that had approached him, knowing that an easy fuck was all she'd wanted. And while it had been his for the taking, a quick hotel-room fuck with a nameless woman would have tempted him when he was a much younger man but now no longer held any appeal. At thirty-two, he wanted more.

His thoughts were interrupted when his phone vibrated. Glancing at the caller ID, he grinned. "Hey, Mom."

When his father had finally retired from the Army, his parents settled in North Carolina on the coast. His dad loved to fish, and his mom enjoyed walking on the beach and her book clubs. For them, it had been good to put down roots after thirty years of temporary homes. "Is everything okay?"

"Everything's fine. Your dad went out with some buddies today and came back with more fish tales than fish, I think. But he was happy, so that's all that counts."

Chuckling, he had no problem imagining his dad having a good time out on the boat with buddies.

"I'll have you know I came home with two fish!" It sounded as though his father called from the other side of the room.

"I guess you can tell I've got you on speaker so that your father can hear as well," his mom said. "How's the trip going?"

"Hey, Dad. I actually stopped at the Air and Space Museum this morning and got to see the type of plane that Grandpa used to fly in the war."

His dad exclaimed in excitement, and they chatted for several minutes about the various planes. His mom, bored with their conversation, cut in, "So, when are you getting to Maine?"

"Maybe sooner than I originally thought. I'm stopping and seeing a few sights, and while I don't mind traveling by myself, I'm really looking forward to getting to the East Coast."

"I know you've always preferred having time to yourself, but I hate for you to drive on such a long trip with no one else for company."

He shook his head slightly at the subtle hint. As soon as he'd turned thirty, his mom had started dropping hints about wanting him to settle down and give her grandchildren.

"It's okay, Mom. I know you worry. But I'm fine with taking things slow. I'm enjoying the drive and listening to a few audiobooks."

His dad piped up from the background and said, "It took me many years to discover that, Son. I was always with others in my platoon, and I wondered if I would be bored in retirement. But I've found that I enjoy spending time with myself."

"I don't mind telling you that I hope this job transfer to Lighthouse Security Investigations will be my last employment change. I'm ready to put down roots, and Wyoming never quite felt like home."

"Hear, hear, to that!" his mom agreed. "I think it's high time you got settled!"

Deciding not to touch that last statement, he chatted for a few more minutes before saying goodbye and tossed his phone to the nightstand. Sliding down in bed, he stared out at the moonlight shining over the undulating water of the Mississippi River. What he told his parents was true… he never minded spending time by himself, but the thought of putting down roots made him wonder if he would always be alone. *But my line of work makes it hard to find the right woman. Someone interesting and yet uncomplicated.* And with that thought, he slept fitfully.

2

After a restless night, a wide yawn split his face the next morning as he set out across Illinois. Following Highway 80, he passed signs for various tourist attractions but didn't feel like sightseeing. He occasionally spied an interesting barn in the distance, but on the interstate, there was no place to pull off for pictures.

The highway passed just south of Chicago, and he stopped for lunch at another diner. Scanning the interior, he sighed at the crowd of families waiting to be seated. Ordering his lunch to go, he munched on his roast beef sandwich while sitting in his SUV but would have preferred eating at a table. *Third day on the road and I'm already over this. Forget adventure... let me just get there.*

Stopping a block down the road at a gas station, he filled his tank and made a quick trip to the men's room. As he paid, he heard another customer complaining about roadwork on the highway in the direction he was going. Asking for more information, he discovered that traffic was not backed up very far, but the idea of sitting in any traffic did not appeal.

Nodding his thanks, he climbed back into his SUV and checked for an alternate route. Discovering that there were several small back roads that he could take for an hour or so that would lead him back to the highway, he made up his mind. *"Sometimes back roads are where we find adventure."* Giving his head a shake, he wondered why he was thinking so much of his grandfather on this trip.

Following his GPS to avoid traffic, he drove along small, two-lane country roads through the farmland of Illinois. Roads that were flat and straight, bordered on either side with green fields and a few forests. Even with little sleep the previous night, Levi began to relax and take in the view. He wasn't passing any of the typical tourist sites but enjoyed the drive, allowing his mind to wander.

His attention was snared at a sight in the distance. Slowing his SUV, he spied a vehicle that appeared to have skidded off the road, the front end now resting downward in a ditch. Continuing to brake, he slowed so that he could get a better look. The small sedan was old, a few rust spots showing on the back bumper that was now sticking up in the air. Passing at a crawl, he discerned a shredded front tire.

A lone woman was standing to the side, looking down at her phone, her long dark hair whipping about in the breeze. Petite, dressed in jeans and a denim jacket, she was of uncertain age. Glancing to the front and behind, Levi observed no other vehicles on the road. He pulled to the shoulder and climbed out of his SUV. Aware that a woman traveling alone would be cautious with a man approaching, he stopped twenty feet away and lifted his hands to the sides. "Are you all right, Miss? Can I call someone for you? Can I help?"

She turned her face toward him at the sound of his voice. She lifted one hand to the crown of her head, grabbing a handful of hair and holding it back from her face. Even from a distance, he could tell she was beautiful.

"Oh, I'm so glad you showed up! I really need help!"

"May I come closer?"

As she nodded, her smile spread across her face. Waving him closer, she dropped the handful of hair and the breeze sent the strands dancing again as the sunlight captured the red highlights in her dark brown hair. "Yes, that's fine."

Continuing to walk forward, he approached slowly, his gaze moving from her over to the vehicle. It was now easy to see it was going to be difficult to pull out of the ditch with the front end crumpled. The airbag had inflated, and he jerked his gaze back to her, scanning her from head to toe. A blue t-shirt with a denim jacket over jeans paired with flat shoes made up her simple outfit. Slightly rumpled, but he ascertained no obvious injuries. "Are you hurt?"

She shook her head as he stepped closer, her dark eyes meeting his. Her skin was clear, with little makeup, although she had dark circles underneath her big, brown eyes. A few little freckles dotted across her upper cheeks, drawing his attention. She was much shorter than he, and as her head tilted back to hold his gaze, he viewed the pale skin of her neck, wondering if it was as soft as it appeared.

"My front tire blew out. The car went into a skid, and I battled to keep it on the road but completely lost control."

Her words jerked his focus back to the situation and off her appearance. His face heated, and he could not remember the last time he'd blushed. Clearing his throat, he stepped closer to her vehicle, seeing it filled with luggage, boxes, and bags. "Were you moving?" As soon as the words left his mouth, he winced, knowing her situation was none of his business. Before he could retract his question, she stepped closer and sighed.

"Actually, yes. I've lived in Chicago for a long time but decided I needed a change of scenery. I'd rented a small, furnished apartment, so when I decided to move, I was able to fit everything into my vehicle."

"Well, we can call for a tow truck, but that's only going to take care of part of the problem. They can tow your car out of the ditch and to a garage, but I'm afraid as old as it is, your insurance will probably just consider it totaled."

She did not respond, and he turned his attention back to her, noting her furrowed brow. Her face held anxiety, and she lifted her gaze back to him.

"I'm not sure what to do," she confessed. "I didn't need a car living in downtown Chicago but kept this oldie from my college days. Now, I can just get rid of it as junk but will need something to drive."

Levi had his phone out and quickly made a call to

roadside assistance. Gaining the number for a local garage, he placed the call, explaining the circumstances and location. Disconnecting, he said, "Okay, we've got someone coming and you can decide what you want to tell them to do. Perhaps they can also take you to where you can get a rental car."

She nodded, the corners of her lips attempting to turn upward but barely managing a tight smile. "Thank you. I was desperately trying to figure out what to do when you came along, and I appreciate your help."

Her gaze darted back and forth along the road, and she nibbled on her bottom lip. Seeing no one, he asked, "Are you expecting someone?"

Barking out a laugh, she shook her head in quick jerks. "No, of course not. I don't know anyone around here." She lifted her gaze as she stepped closer and extended her hand. "I'm Claire, by the way. Claire Loman."

Clasping her smaller hand in his own, he felt the warmth in her grip. "It's nice to meet you, Claire. I'm Levi Amory."

She nibbled her lip again and his gaze was riveted to the reddened flesh, finding her plump lips to be distracting.

She let go of her lip to heave a sigh, grabbing her hair again to keep it from blowing into her face. "Um... I'm sure you probably have somewhere to be. I hate to keep you, but..."

"Don't worry about it. I'm on my own schedule and wouldn't feel right leaving you here to deal with the tow company by yourself. If it's okay with you, I'd like to stick around to make sure everything's okay."

Her relief was evident as her shoulders sagged and air rushed from her lungs. "Oh, thank you, Levi."

What he told her was the truth—he was on his own schedule, and in the time they'd been together, no other vehicle had come down the road. "If you feel safe with me, why don't we wait in my SUV? You can keep the passenger door open, but I've got water and some snacks."

Her eyes widened with interest, and she nodded. "That sounds good. I was so busy packing up this morning that I skipped breakfast."

"It's actually past lunchtime."

She blinked at his pronouncement and shook her head slightly. "I hadn't even noticed. I'm afraid it's been a rather... um... trying couple of days."

Making sure not to crowd her, he led the way back to his SUV and opened the door for her. Walking around, he climbed into the driver's seat and reached for the water bottles and cheese crackers. Glad to see that she was comfortable enough to climb into the passenger seat, she did keep the door open. She drank thirstily and quickly finished the pack of crackers.

"Thank you so much for this."

Before he had a chance to respond, the rumble of a diesel engine sounded in the distance, and they watched as a tow truck approached. She sucked in an audible inhalation, and he turned to the side. "Claire, are you okay?"

Once again, he could see the forced smile on her

face. "I really hate being the damsel in distress, but I feel a little out of my element. I'm embarrassed, but I don't know anything about cars. Mine was just sitting in a parking garage for most of the past years, and I only drove it occasionally."

"Let's go together. I'll stay out of it unless you need my help or my opinion. Is that okay?"

"Yes, that's perfect!" Once again, relief flooded her face as her smile widened.

His hand lifted slightly, then halted suddenly when he realized he was reaching up to cup her face. He blinked, stunned at his impromptu movement, but there was something about Claire that drew his attention. She easily admitted when she needed help and didn't mind offering thanks when warranted. Her gaze dropped to his hand hovering between them and he moved it quickly.

She blushed before hopping out of his SUV, and he rolled his eyes at his lack of finesse. They walked back toward her car as the tow truck driver parked and swung down to the ground. The older man smiled as he walked forward, his hand stuck out. "I'm George. Let's see what you've got here."

Levi stayed close to make sure that she was not being taken advantage of, but, as far as he could tell, the mechanic was giving her good information.

"I agree that your insurance company is going to total this old girl," George said, patting the trunk of the car sticking up in the air. "You've decided you just want it junked, right?"

"Yes, it sounds like it can't be repaired, certainly not

for what it's worth." Claire looked up at George, her top teeth worrying her bottom lip. "Is it worth the price of you just towing it away for me?"

George's eyebrows lifted. "Ma'am, I can sell it for junk for more than what it'll cost me to tow it off. I don't want to take advantage of you."

"I appreciate that, but it would be worth it to me to have you tow it away and deal with it. I'd rather not have any… well, I'd just like to be rid of it. And can you take me into town so that I can get a rental car?"

George's gaze moved between Claire's and Levi's as he rubbed his hand over his stubbled jaw. "Ma'am, I'm afraid there isn't a rental car place anywhere around here."

Levi watched her face fall and inwardly battled. Not one to normally deviate from his plan, he couldn't imagine what it was about this woman that made him offer to give her a lift. *A woman alone, taking a ride from a man she doesn't know. Hell, it's not smart for me to offer a ride to a woman I don't know!*

Her lips were pinched tightly together, and he could see thoughts working behind her eyes. Before changing his mind, he quickly offered, "If you feel safe with me, we can load your things into my SUV, and I'll get you to a rental facility. I just left the FBI and have identification with me." As soon as the words left his mouth, he once again wondered why he made the outrageous suggestion, but he pulled out his driver's license and handed it to her.

She held his gaze quietly for a long moment, then stared at his ID. He wondered if she was going to turn him down. Finally, nodding, she smiled. "Thank you, Levi. I hate to take advantage of you even more, but I don't seem to have a choice." She dug into her purse and pulled out her driver's license along with an ID badge showing she was an employee of Martins & Lee Investment.

He jogged to his SUV, ignoring the relief he felt at her acceptance. He had hated the idea that Claire would be stuck in a small town with no transportation. Backing up his SUV and U-Haul, he stopped close to her vehicle.

Shifting a few items around, they were able to cram her bags and boxes into his SUV. She signed the paperwork George produced, giving him title to her vehicle and the agreement that it would just be junked. With handshakes and a wave, they left George to do his work. Once inside and buckled up, he turned toward her and asked, "You ready?"

The lines of tension on her face had softened and she nodded. "As ready as I'll ever be."

With that, he pulled back onto the little road, eastward bound.

3

"So, it looks like you're moving as well. Where did you come from, and where are you going?"

Claire had twisted slightly so that she was staring at him, and Levi glanced to the side. Her eager expression gave evidence that she was asking out of interest and not just filling up silence. "I'm changing jobs, so I've left Wyoming and relocating to Maine."

"Wow, that's quite a distance!" She glanced to the back toward the U-Haul, then turned her attention to him again. "Were you able to get everything into your U-Haul?"

"I left my sofa and bed, which were my biggest pieces of furniture. I figure I can buy those once I get to Maine."

Nodding, she sighed. "Yeah, when you decide to change scenery, it's amazing what you can truly leave behind."

Her comment sounded cryptic, but he didn't ask for clarification. *We'll just be in each other's company for a little while. No need to make things more complicated than they already are.*

As they continued down the small country road, an old, red-painted barn became visible. His foot fell from the accelerator, and he pulled to the side of the road. "Sorry, this'll just take a moment."

"What's up?"

"I like to take pictures of old barns. I've taken a couple on this trip but not as many as I thought I would."

Before his words were finished, she threw open her door and climbed out of his SUV. They walked to the fence together, and he snapped several photos.

As they walked back, she asked, "Are you a photographer?"

He snorted and shook his head. "I don't have an artistic bone in my body. But for some reason, old barns appeal to my sense of stability, I suppose. Anyway, it's a habit I started years ago, and whenever I see a picturesque barn, if I'm able, I stop and snap a picture."

"Well, I'll keep my eyes peeled in case I see another good one."

He started to say that there was no need since they'd soon come to a town where she could get a rental car, but the words halted in his throat. Even though he knew nothing about Claire, it wasn't awkward to have her in the car with him. Muttering, "Thanks," he pulled back onto the road.

"Wildflowers were my dad's thing," she said, her voice soft as though memories were floating past.

He remained quiet, hoping she would explain.

"When I was little, we'd take weekends to get out of the suburbs. We'd drive on little country roads like this, and my dad would stop and pull out his camera to snap pictures of wildflowers." She chuckled and shook her head. "Funny, but I haven't thought about that in ages. But then, it's been a long time since I've been on a back road."

"So, have you lived in Chicago for a while?"

"Sort of. I was actually born and raised outside Chicago in the suburbs. Both my parents were teachers, and when they retired, they decided to travel. They're currently in the south of France."

"So, you work for a Chicago investment company, but you're moving to the East Coast?"

"Yeah. Um... I needed a change of scenery."

"From people or your job?"

She snorted. "A little of both, I suppose."

"Did you have a particular place you were going?"

"I thought perhaps Boston."

Unable to keep the surprise out of his voice, he asked, "You *thought*?"

Her hands were in her lap, fingers clasped tightly together, and her brow was once again furrowed. "Yeah." She let out a deep sigh. "I confess that my leaving Chicago was rather impromptu. I had my reasons, but my plans are a bit... fluid at this point."

He glanced at the GPS, trying to discern what to do. His original plan was to get back up on the highway as soon as possible but was uncertain if there was a town with a rental car business before he got to the highway. He approached an intersection and flipped on his blinker. "I'm afraid with the U-Haul I have to stop for gas more often."

"Oh, that's not a problem. I could use a trip to the ladies' room, anyway." She opened her purse and pulled out her wallet. "I'm going to get some snacks and can pay for the gas."

Shaking his head, he replied, "Don't worry about it. I was going to have to get gas whether I had another passenger or not." She smiled, and his gaze followed her as she went inside the small store. Leaning against his SUV as the gas was pumping, he fought an inner battle. He could offer her a ride to Boston since it was on his way, and yet, she was a stranger. Closing his eyes for a moment, he leaned his head back and let the sun warm his face.

"You look comfortable."

Hearing her voice so close, he dropped his chin and saw her standing nearby, her hands full of drinks, chips, and granola bars. The tension lines in her face had relaxed and her true beauty beamed. Good at reading people, he felt certain she was exactly what she presented... a woman in need with no ulterior motive.

Climbing back inside, he pulled away from the gas pump but did not turn onto the road. Cutting off the engine, he shifted toward her and said, "Let's talk about what to do from here."

She glanced out the window before turning her attention back to him, tilting her head to the side. "Oh... um... okay."

"While you were in the store, I was checking our options. There doesn't appear to be another town on this little road for a while that has a car rental facility. I had originally planned to take this road just to get around the construction that was on the highway. This'll put us on the east side of South Bend, and it'll be about a hundred more miles to Toledo. By the time we get there, we can find a car rental facility." He watched her face carefully, searching for nuances to see how she was taking his information.

Her shoulders relaxed and she smiled. "Oh, that's fine, Levi. You had me worried. I was afraid you were ready to leave me on the side of the road."

"Never! My mama raised me better than that."

"Glad to hear it." She reached over and placed her hand on his. The warmth from her fingers traveled up his arm and his breath quickened. Her gaze landed on their connection before she pulled her hand back, a blush crossing her face again. Swallowing deeply, she added, "I can't think of a better idea, so I really appreciate you helping me out."

Feeling strangely relieved, he restarted the engine and pulled onto the road. It didn't take long to come to the entrance ramp taking them back onto the highway. Traffic was still light, and he settled into a steady speed. She twisted the cap off a soda and passed it to him before getting one for herself.

"You didn't have to buy snacks for me."

She laughed, the sound delightful to his ears. "Snacks are imperative for car trips."

"Yeah?" he asked, lifting an eyebrow.

She nodded while taking a bite of her granola bar. "Absolutely." After several minutes of munching, she twisted to look at him. "So, I'm assuming the career you left behind was with the FBI? Or are you just changing offices?"

"It's actually a career change. I decided to work for a private security company."

"Wow, that's interesting. Is that what you wanted to do?"

He hesitated, unused to talking about himself. A snort erupted, and he said, "Actually, I think I must be a work in progress. I've had several careers." He cringed at his words, thinking it made him sound like he could not make up his mind.

"I can understand that," she enthused. "I think it's hard to find the one perfect job. Most of us settle for something that pays the bills, and then we just make the most of it."

He nodded and felt her gaze on him, but instead of feeling scrutinized, it seemed that she understood.

"What other jobs have you had?" she asked.

He glanced toward her, but before he had a chance to speak, she rushed, "I really want to know. You don't have to tell me anything, but I am interested."

"I was always interested in history, but, after an Associate's Degree, I joined the Army."

"The Army?"

"My dad was in the Army. I can't say it was always my dream to follow in his footsteps, but I didn't want to teach history and really had no idea what I wanted to do." He shrugged, adding, "I became a Ranger, but after six years decided to get out. I had a friend that was in the FBI and made the jump. Now, six years later, I'm giving up on government work and going private." Glancing at her again, he asked, "What about you?"

She puffed out a breath and grimaced. "I had no idea what I wanted to do in school but majored in finance. I was good at it, but I can't say that it was my first love. When you get out of college, you need to have a job so that you can become an *independent adult*." She laughed as she emphasized the last two words. "But when you attain that status, it isn't always as glamorous as you hoped it would be. But, by then, there were bills to pay, so I stayed."

"And now you're leaving it?"

Her smile remained, but it no longer reached her eyes. "Well, let's just say that I'm leaving Chicago. I felt the urge to get out and go somewhere new. Start over. The timing was right… but the vehicle was wrong!"

A burst of laughter erupted from him, and he couldn't remember the last time that had happened. Shaking his head as his mirth slowed, he said, "I'd say you're right."

For the next hour and a half, they laughed and talked, and he enjoyed the companionship. Claire was smart, articulate, and it didn't hurt that her smile was the brightest thing he'd seen in a long time.

The highway ran south of Toledo, but Claire was already on her phone starting to call car rental facilities. After her third call she finished with, "Thank you for trying," he turned and looked toward her.

"What's going on?"

"I can't believe this. I can't find any rentals. It seems that this weekend there's a national political rally in

Toledo, a country music festival that's pulling in some of the top musicians, a state-wide automobile show, and a 10K race. I'm not sure Toledo has ever had so much going on all at one time." She slumped back in her seat and sighed heavily. "These were the ones that were closest to the highway and near the airport. Let me start looking out a little bit."

"Look, Claire, I had an idea earlier but figured it was crazy. I was going to stop just on the other side of Toledo for the night. We can get a couple of hotel rooms, and you can decide what you'd like to do. If you want to stay in Toledo for a couple of days and get a rental car when one is available, that's fine. If you'd like to continue heading east with me tomorrow, I'm game."

"Levi, that's a huge imposition."

He heard hope in her words in spite of the air of denial. "I have to admit that I'm used to traveling alone, but your company today has been really nice. Look, I don't expect you to decide right now. I know you're overwhelmed and tired, so why don't we stop at a hotel? Have dinner. And you can rest and let me know in the morning if you'd like to stay or continue on with me."

"All the way to Boston?"

He hefted his shoulders in a shrug. "I'm practically going right past Boston on my way to Maine."

She sucked in her lips as though she was trying to hide her smile, but her relief was palpable. Nodding, she replied, "All right. That actually sounds like a good idea. We'll stop for the night, eat, and then I can make up my mind. One way or the other, maybe we can have breakfast in the morning, and I can let you know."

He grinned, and they continued on the highway for about fifteen more miles, finding an exit with several hotels. Choosing one with a restaurant next door, he parked but noticed the parking lot was full. Hoping they'd be able to find two rooms, they walked side by side into the lobby and approached the receptionist counter.

"We need two rooms, please," he said.

The receptionist glanced between them and nodded. "You're in luck because we're almost full. I do have two rooms, but they're not next to each other."

"That's fine," he said, pulling out his credit card.

Claire's brow furrowed as she handed her card to the receptionist also, then drummed her fingers on top of the counter until it was returned to her.

Noting her unease and unable to keep his investigative mind from clicking, Levi managed to see the name on the card, ascertaining that it was her debit card. *Perhaps it has a limit, and she's afraid of overspending.*

Leaning down, he whispered, "Don't worry about extra charges on your card unless you decide to call China in the middle of the night or pretend to be a rock star and trash the room." Her face softened as a smile replaced the frown. He smiled in return, surprised at how much he liked seeing that look on her face.

Once they had their room keys, he walked her around the building to room A211 and made sure she was inside securely. "My room is on the other side. B117. First floor. Take your time and rest. How about we meet in the lobby in about thirty minutes and walk to dinner?" Gaining her acquiescence, he watched as she closed the door before heading to his room.

Stretching out on the bed, he stared at the ceiling. Thinking about the events of the day, he snorted ruefully. For a man who was rarely impulsive and thought carefully through each decision, his day had been one big impetuous action after the other. Getting off the highway and taking the back roads. Offering to drive a stranger. Then offering to let her travel all the way to Boston with him.

He pressed the heels of his palms into his eyes for a moment and shook his head slowly, wondering what had gotten into him. *Claire. Fresh-faced, beautiful, funny Claire.* Glancing at the time, he hurried back out to the lobby, ready for dinner, realizing the bottom line was he liked her company. *And it sure as hell beats eating alone.*

4

"So, blowing up the pottery kiln was the last time I tried an art class. Even with my mother as a teacher, she encouraged me to develop other pursuits!"

Levi laughed along with Claire as she finished her story and they pushed their empty plates away. She waved her hands around in animation when she talked, her eyes bright and her smile wide. He could not remember the last time he'd enjoyed a meal so much.

When she'd walked into the lobby of the hotel, his feet had stuttered to a halt. She was still wearing jeans but had changed into a dark green blouse that complemented her pale complexion and smattering of freckles. Somehow, she managed to look drop-dead gorgeous and wholesome at the same time.

The server came by to see if they wanted coffee after their dessert, but they both declined. "I'm afraid I didn't sleep all that great last night," he confided. "If I have coffee it really will be a bad night."

Nodding, she agreed, stifling a yawn. "I can only

have coffee in the morning, and that's to get my eyes open. I know a lot of people drink it at night, but I'd never get to sleep."

As the server came again with their bill, he pulled out his card. Watching Claire dig into her purse for her wallet, he said, "No, please. This is my treat."

"I know that I should graciously accept your offer, but Levi, you've done so much for me already."

"Nothing that I wouldn't be doing by myself. This dinner was my suggestion anyway, so it's my treat."

Her hand darted out to rest on his arm. Leaning forward, she held his gaze. "Thank you so much." She sucked in a ragged breath and let it out slowly, still holding his gaze. "You've taken what was a disastrous day and made it so much better."

Tiny electric jolts moved up his arm, emanating from her warm touch. Unable to look away from her dark-eyed gaze, he sat, entranced. Laughter from another table startled both of them, and she jerked her hand back, her top teeth landing on her bottom lip as though to keep from smiling. He noted she was unsuccessful as her lips curved upward.

As they walked toward the hotel, a breeze blew and he battled the desire to place his arm protectively around her shoulders. She had grown quiet, and his mind turned toward her nebulous plans. "So, once you get to Boston, do you already have a place picked out to move into?"

"Um... no. Not really. Well, not at all." Her eyes cut toward him before she looked back down at the sidewalk. "I've got a friend that lives there, but I haven't heard back from her. I can stay in a hotel for a few nights until I can find a place to live."

"Do you have a job already lined up?"

She sucked in her lips, and the corners turned up in a halfhearted smile. "Sure. I mean, who would pick up and move to a new city without a plan?"

He didn't ask any more questions but observed her hands fiddling with her purse strap. A rueful snort slipped from her. "I'd planned on making the move, but, well, just not right now. So, this is a little impromptu. But it'll be fine."

He wasn't sure if she was trying to convince him or herself, but nerves were flowing from her, encircling them, choking off the previously easy conversation. Arriving at the hotel, they stopped outside her room. Her hands were still clutching her purse, but she looked up and offered a little smile.

"So, breakfast tomorrow?" she asked, her brows lifted and her eyes wide.

"Absolutely. Is seven o'clock too early?"

A quick shake of her head sent her hair flying about her shoulders. "No. That's fine. I'm an early riser and know you want to get on the road."

"Okay, we'll meet in the lobby at seven, have breakfast, and then you can let me know what you'd like to do." He wanted to encourage her to continue the trip with him, but something was off. And, not knowing what that was made him hesitate. His hands twitched at his sides, longing to reach out to her. Clearing his throat, he said, "I'll see you tomorrow. Sleep tight, Claire."

With a nod and a wave, she went inside her room, and he heard the lock on the door click. Heading straight to his room, he went inside but couldn't settle. He began to pace, wondering if he was doing the right thing by offering her a ride. *What do I really know about her? Abso-fucking-lutely nothing! She could be a con artist... an opportunist... who the hell knows? Or maybe she's just down on her luck.*

Finally, giving in to the inner battle tormenting him, he pulled out his phone and punched a few buttons before changing his mind. "Tate? Jesus, I hate to call you this late, but is there any way I can find out about someone?"

"Sure. Actually, several of us are still at LSI, checking on one of the Keepers' missions. What's going on?"

"I was wondering if I can get a little background on someone. Claire Loman from Chicago." He gave Tate a quick explanation of how he met her, then gave him the name of the investment firm she worked with as well as the tags from the car she had been driving.

"No problem. Josh says this shouldn't take long."

While waiting to hear back, he took a shower, rinsing away the sweat and fatigue of the day. Pulling on a pair of boxers and sweatpants, he stared into the mirror after swiping at the condensation. *What are you doing, man? You like her, and she trusts you... and now you're checking up on her.* His phone vibrated with an incoming text, and he looked down to see it was from Tate.

Sorry. We got involved in something else. Josh is starting to look now.

Levi yawned, tired from the day, and was now

regretting having involved LSI in checking on Claire. He shook his head and winced. *Jesus, I haven't even had my first day employed with them, and I'm already asking for a favor. Claire is just going through a life change, and I've let my suspicions take over my good sense.* His finger hesitated over his phone, wanting to tell Tate that he changed his mind.

Before he had a chance to begin typing, his phone rang.

"Tate, I'm really sorry I asked you all to do this—"

"No, no, don't worry about it," Tate assured. "Believe me, as Keepers, we all pitch in whenever we can. Plus, Josh pulled some interesting information that you'll want to know about."

His stomach fell. "Yeah?"

"Claire Loman has been employed by Martins and Lee Investment for the past four years. Before that, she worked in a bank."

"So, she's who she says she is?"

"Yes, but... her employment was terminated two days ago. There's been no police report, but, according to an internal email from one of the senior partners to a junior partner, she's being looked into for embezzling money. It appears that over five hundred thousand dollars has gone missing from one of the client's accounts that she was handling."

Sitting straight up, his heart pounded. "You're kidding me?"

"I take it you didn't get that feeling from her?"

"No... but then... hell, I just met her. Who the fuck knows what she's really like?"

"We find it interesting that they haven't contacted the authorities yet, but then, they may be trying to handle this internally. Who the fuck knows why some businesses make the decisions they do?"

His mind raced, and he appreciated the quiet moment Tate gave him to process the information.

"What are you going to do?" Tate asked.

"Since no police report has been filed, I've got no reason to contact them. But I also don't want her traveling with me. I'll tell her in the morning that I've had a change of plans, and she'll need to find her own way to Boston."

"Sorry as fuck, man," Tate said. "So far, your trip hasn't turned out the way you were hoping."

"No worries. It's still been a good trip, and I have to admit her company was nice. Broke up the monotony for a while, but I've never minded traveling by myself. I'll hit the road in the morning after I have a chance to talk to her. After all this, I'll probably head on straight to Maine. I'll see you in a couple of days." With good-byes, they disconnected.

He tossed his book to the nightstand, blowing out his breath in a long sigh. He had enjoyed Claire's company but was no longer sorry he had LSI check into her. *Shit.* He scrubbed his hand over his face, thinking about the uncomfortable conversation he would have to have in the morning. Turning off the light, he slid under the covers and closed his eyes. But, for the second night in a row, sleep came fitfully.

The next morning, Levi arrived at the lobby early, but, after a moment of pacing, decided he didn't want to put off the inevitable any longer. Walking around the building to her room, he came to her door and lifted his hand to knock, halting when he saw that her door was opened about half an inch. He hesitated, hearing a man's voice inside. *Shit, she's got someone in there? When the hell did she meet them?*

He started to step back, but the idea of just sending her a text saying that he was leaving felt disingenuous. Lifting his hand again to knock after deciding to confront her, he jolted as the man's voice could now be clearly heard.

"We're leaving here now. You call out or step one fucking toe out of line and you're dead."

His heart jolted, but training kicked in and he instantly assessed the situation. Grimacing at not having a service revolver with him, he shifted slightly, moving to the side, and waited. The door opened and Claire stumbled out, her face pale and hands shaking. The man behind her, obviously not expecting trouble since his hands were down at his sides, never saw Levi coming. With a swift kick and punch, the man crumpled soundlessly to the floor, his gun knocked out of his hand.

Claire whirled, her dark eyes wide and mouth open. "Levi! Oh, thank God!"

Levi secured the man's weapon, dragging him back into the room. Standing with his hands on his hips, he leveled her with his glare. "I gotta deal with him, but you stay in the room. When I finish, it'll be time to start talking, Claire, because I wanna know what the fuck is going on!"

She opened her mouth then snapped it closed again, nodding. She plopped down on the edge of the bed, her hands clasped in her lap and her gaze following his movements. He pulled the wallet, phone, and keys out of the man's pocket, and, standing at the door, he pressed the fob, glad the man's car was directly outside her room. He made a quick picture of the driver's license, then put the wallet back into the man's pocket.

Jogging out, he opened the back door of the car, then hefted the man over his shoulder in a fireman's hold, and with a quick look up and down the sidewalk and seeing no one, he carried him directly to the car and dumped him into the back seat. Keeping the phone and keys, he walked back into the room.

"Get your stuff."

Claire stood and lifted her hands. "Levi, I promise I can explain—"

"Oh, you're going to explain, sweetheart, but we don't have time right now. I'm taking you with me. So, get your stuff."

Glad she didn't argue, he watched as she grabbed her overnight bag and purse, did a quick scan of the bathroom and room, then hurried to stand in front of him. They walked briskly around the building and climbed into his SUV. He ran to get his bag and was back within minutes.

As soon as they were on the road, he said, "Okay. Start talking. And I'll warn you, I've got ways of checking. So make sure it's the truth."

5

Claire stared out of the passenger window, the view a blur as she blinked away the tears that were forming in her eyes. She lifted a shaky hand and pressed it against her temple in an attempt to rub away the pounding in her head. *Was it only a week ago that my life was normal? Average? Even boring?* And now, on the run, with no real plan in place, she had no idea where her life was going.

Yesterday, stuck on the side of the road, she couldn't believe how her horrible luck changed when Levi approached. Tall, dark, dressed in jeans and a tight navy t-shirt showcasing muscles. For a millisecond, she'd focused on the loose-limbed walk of confidence he had, then noticed the way he held his hands up slightly. *He didn't want me to be afraid.* And after being terrified for the past day, it was nice to have a few seconds to just enjoy the vision walking toward her.

And his offer to assist was so kind she felt guilty that she didn't explain her predicament. *But how would I tell a stranger that someone might be after me... including the police?*

As the day progressed, it was easier to see him as the proverbial knight on a white horse. Not one to give over to flights of fancy, her imaginings still seemed apropos as their conversation was easy on the road. And the reality was that dinner with him last night was better than any date she'd ever been on. Lying in bed last night, she'd gone to sleep with thoughts of the possibility they might stay in touch beyond Boston. *If I was able to prove my innocence and not end up in prison.*

She was so sure it was Levi when she heard the knock on her door this morning, she didn't even look out first. Throwing open the door, she was stunned when the burly man forced his way in and pointed a gun at her. *A gun... oh, God... I've never even seen a gun up close.* Her chest depressed as the air rushed from her lungs, remembering the stone-cold fear staring at the weapon.

As soon as he asked for what she'd taken, she knew exactly why he was there. Closing her eyes for a moment, she could still feel the helplessness as he forced her out of the room and the hopefulness when Levi suddenly lunged from the side, disarming the man and knocking him unconscious.

The sound of his throat clearing jerked her back to her present situation—in a vehicle with a seriously pissed-off man who had every right to be pissed off. Turning back toward the front of the vehicle, she was very aware of Levi. Her rescuer with dark hair and dark eyes, a brooding expression in place until he smiled, and then his face lit with warmth. But now, that warmth was replaced with angry vibes directed at her. So hot she was uncertain how her skin was not seared.

Cutting her eyes to the side, she could see the tension in his hands as he drove, and yet he was waiting, giving her a chance to explain. She sucked in a ragged breath and her shoulders slumped as exhaustion weighed heavily.

Without looking toward him, she licked her dry lips and began. "Everything I told you is true. My name is Claire Loman, and I worked for Martins and Lee Investment. It was a midsize firm with about twenty-five employees, sixteen of those investors, like myself. After four years, I was no longer the newest hire but had proven that I could handle my clients. I liked my job well enough, my coworkers, my bosses. Everything was fine until a week ago."

Casting her mind back to the previous week, she sat silent, trying to discern the exact moment everything began to fall apart.

"And?"

The one word from Levi cut through her thoughts and she startled. Lifting her hand to her forehead again, she mumbled, "Sorry. It's all so overwhelming."

He didn't say anything else, so she continued. "One of my coworkers was in a car accident and landed in the hospital. It wasn't life-threatening, but he did need surgery and was going to be out for weeks. Mr. Martins said that he'd take over Perry's accounts until he came back. I thought it was a little strange for a senior partner to take over the accounts of a junior investor, but it didn't have anything to do with me, so I didn't give it another thought. Then, suddenly, Mr. Martins was called out of town for a family funeral right when some of Perry's accounts needed reviewing. My direct supervisor asked me to handle it. That was a week ago."

She leaned her head against the headrest and closed her eyes. *I'm so tired. So fuckin' tired.*

"You haven't rested at all in the past week."

Realizing she'd spoken aloud, a rueful snort slipped out as she shook her head. After a moment, she chanced another glance to the side and stared at Levi's profile. Strong jaw with dark stubble. It was hard not to have fantasized about what his stubble would feel like against her skin. *Now I'll never get the chance to know what it would be like to be held by a man like him.*

When he'd turned his intense gaze toward her yesterday, she felt as though she had all his attention. She still did but knew it was because he wanted information. She couldn't blame him; after all, he'd incapacitated a man and saved her this morning. Finally, answering his question, she replied, "No. Sleep has been elusive as things went from curious to bad to worse."

Her stomach growled loudly, and he shot his eagle-eyed stare over toward her. They hadn't had breakfast, but she wasn't about to ask him to stop somewhere. As far as she was concerned, the further away from Chicago they got, the better it was for her. She reached into her purse and pulled out a pack of cheese crackers left over from yesterday. Ripping them open, she handed several to him, grateful when he reached out and took them. Unscrewing the top on a fresh bottle of water, she handed that to him as well before getting one for herself.

After a moment of nibbling to ease the hunger, she took a long sip of water. Wiping her mouth, she screwed the top back onto the bottle and sighed. "I stayed late after doing my own work so that I could review Perry's accounts. Everything looked to be in order except for one. That one account simply did not add up. At first glance, there was nothing wrong with it, but, because it was so similar to one of my accounts, I couldn't figure out why Perry's numbers were off by five hundred thousand dollars. By the time I went home that evening, I had convinced myself that I was simply tired and needed fresh eyes to look at it the next day."

"I take it the next day it didn't look any clearer?"

"No. There were withdrawals from one client's account and the paper trail led into a virtual forest of companies, none of them part of our portfolios. By the third day, my suspicions were heightened but I didn't know who to trust. You see, each of those withdrawals and company investments were signed off by not only Perry but Mr. Martins."

"They were embezzling."

She noted Levi had made a statement, not a question. Nodding slowly, she said, "The evidence was in front of me, but I didn't want to accept it. And then I didn't know what to do about it. If I was misinterpreting and made an accusation that was wrong, I could lose my job or be buried as a junior investor for the rest of my career. But, if I wasn't misinterpreting, then I was looking at embezzlement by not only a junior investor but a senior partner. Plus, I didn't know who to go to. Did I bring it to my supervisor? Did I go straight to Mr. Lee? Did I go to the authorities? I had no clue what to do."

A sigh of air rushed from her lungs and the weight on her shoulders seemed to intensify. "I thought I had another day to take one last look at things before Mr. Martins came back. But he showed up at work, made a beeline into my tiny office, and, with a big smile on his face, thanked me for assisting but told me that I was no longer responsible for any of Perry's accounts. The way he was acting… the way he was staring at me… I knew my suspicions were right. So, I did the only thing I could do at the moment and that was slap a big smile on my face and simply agree."

Munching on another cracker, she washed it down with water. So far, Levi was listening with little interruption, but she had no idea what he thought of her story. Afraid that his patience might wane and he would decide to drive her straight to a police station, she continued.

"By the end of the day, I was a nervous wreck. I knew something wasn't right. I knew Mr. Martins, as well as Perry, was involved. I knew it was obvious to Mr. Martins that I'd gone through the accounts. I planned on staying late yesterday, but he showed up at my desk and said that I should take the afternoon off since I'd been pulling double duty with Perry out. I felt like it was a ruse to get me out of the office, but what excuse did I have?"

"What happened next?"

"A stroke of luck." She watched as Levi's unflappable demeanor fell away and his head jerked to the side to stare at her. Quickly explaining, she said, "On my way home, I stopped by my bank to get some cash. Imagine my surprise when I looked at my balance and discovered an extra five hundred thousand dollars sitting in my account."

"Fuck."

Another snort erupted as she agreed. "My thoughts exactly. It didn't take a genius to figure out that Mr. Martins knew I must've looked at everything and he was afraid I'd go to the authorities. Because I have direct deposit with my paycheck, it was not difficult for him to be able to put the money in there."

"So, you ran."

"Yes. I ran."

"What was your plan?"

She lifted her shoulders in a little shrug and shook her head. "All I wanted to do was get away. I had no idea what Mr. Martins' plans were for me. Call the police and claim that I had embezzled? Maybe keep me under his thumb with the threat hanging over my head? For all I knew that's what had happened to Perry. So, I got home, packed everything I could into my car, and hit the road yesterday morning. I thought if I could disappear for a little while until I had a chance to figure things out, I'd be safe."

Levi was quiet for another moment, and Claire decided she was too exhausted to keep talking. She let the silence move around them, finding her eyelids growing heavy.

"If everything you're telling me is true, why was that man in your room this morning, threatening you?"

Rolling her head to the side, she once more stared at Levi. If men were described in romance novels as tall, dark, and handsome, she'd never truly understood that description until she laid eyes on him. A woman alone with a disabled vehicle should have been very afraid, but fear was not what she felt. If the truth was known, a bolt of lust hit her as he approached. But, with his hands held out in plain sight, his past as an FBI agent, and his offer to help, she tamped down her lust and focused on the warm ease that moved through her at being rescued. With everything that had happened, she hadn't even thanked Levi for saving her.

Sighing her millionth sigh that morning, she replied, "I have a copy of all Perry's dealings. I know that I should never have taken client account information out of the office, but as soon as I discovered discrepancies, I wanted backup. Mr. Martins must have discovered that I have the records. That's why he didn't call the authorities and try to blame the embezzlement on me. Instead, he sent someone after me."

Turning to face him more fully, she added, "I'm ashamed that I didn't even thank you for what you did this morning. But it's now hitting me... you placed yourself in danger. I think the best thing you can do is to pull off at the next exit and let me out. Right now, Levi, you're in danger because of me."

"Did you get all of that?" he asked.

Looking at him sharply, she had no idea what he was

asking her. Before she had a chance to say anything, a male voice coming from his phone replied.

"Got it. Checking out her story now."

She gasped, opening her mouth then snapping it closed as her gaze dropped to his phone as though she would be able to see who now knew her secrets. Levi obviously had called someone and had them on the line the entire time she was speaking. Her stomach clenched as she wondered who now knew that money was in her account and what they were going to do with that information. Her hands began to shake, a combination of anger and nerves, and her heart pounded a drumbeat so loud it was all she could hear.

"Claire. Claire!"

Hearing her name, her body jolted. "What?"

"You went pale, and I wasn't sure you were breathing. Don't pass out on me now."

With everything that had happened, it was ridiculous to be angry at him, and yet anger was the only emotion she could identify. "You didn't tell me someone was listening."

"Nope."

"Why not? I was talking to *you*, not just anyone. I'm trying to stay safe while figuring all this out, and I don't even know who was listening to this information—"

"*I'm* the one trying to keep you safe. *I'm* the one that disarmed that man this morning. *I'm* the one who needs all the information to figure out what to do. And that started by me finding out what you're involved in. And if I can trust you."

She wanted to argue with his words but couldn't.

Everything he said was true. Pinching her lips together, she turned and looked out her window. She had not been paying attention to the highway signs and had no idea how far they had driven. Doubt slowly wormed its way into her mind as she realized she had no idea who Levi truly was. Maybe he just wanted—

"Don't go there. I can tell that right now you're doubting everything you've told me. But, Claire, if what you told me is the truth, I can help by looking into this mess."

"It's true. It's all true."

She had no idea what kind of *looking into* he meant, but, considering it was more than what she had, she was willing to go on a little faith.

6

The entire time that Claire offered her explanation, Levi had listened carefully. Not only to her words but also her body language while multitasking by focusing on his driving. It was easy to see she was exhausted, and while he had a lot of experience with sleepless nights, he wanted to keep on the road, pushing forward. Whatever was going to happen, they needed to get far away from a possible risk.

At the hotel, once she was secure in his SUV, he'd run back to his room to grab his gear—and call LSI. Giving a quick explanation of what happened, he told the Keepers he would put them on speaker once he got her talking.

Now, he glanced to the side and saw that her eyes were closed, her eyelashes forming dark crescents resting on her cheeks. Her face was pale, even her freckles.

Ever since he first met her, his emotions had run through the gamut. Concern over her car accident had morphed into interest. By the time they had traveled together and had dinner, his interest had moved into possibilities. After discovering the news that she'd left her employment under a cloud, he dismissed all thoughts of wanting to get to know her further. Then, seeing her threatened had kicked in his protective instincts. And now, hearing and believing her story, he wanted nothing more than to make sure she was okay. *Hell, she's a lot braver than I gave her credit for.*

His phone vibrated and he held it to his ear as he answered, wanting to keep the conversation private. "You've got me. Go ahead." He recognized Tate's voice and kept his eyes on the road as he listened.

"Initial information shows that what she's told you could be right. The car belongs to the man in the room, registered to Clarence Tolsen, same name as the driver's license you provided. Digging into him, he's a small town heavy for a bookie in Chicago. Looks like he likes to take jobs on the side, and I can see where five thousand dollars was recently deposited into his bank account from a business buried in paperwork but eventually owned by Mark Martins. Now, what that doesn't tell us is why. Maybe she actually stole the money and Martins sent someone after it. But then, if that were the case, an honest businessman would have contacted the authorities."

Claire's body was still reposed against the car seat, but her breathing had changed, and he knew she was awake, listening to his side of the conversation.

"Copy that."

"We checked the cameras at the hotel and can see

him going into the hotel lobby to make a phone call." Chuckling, Tate added, "He didn't look happy."

A grin slipped over Levi's lips as well in spite of their situation.

Tate continued, "As soon as you stop, scan whatever she's got if it's a hard copy or email it to the secure address I'll send to you. The sooner Josh can start going through that, the sooner we can see what we're up against."

"Copy that. We passed Cleveland, and I'd like to make it to Erie before we stop. We're both pretty tired and hungry, and we'll take a break there. It looks like it's a little over eight hours to get from Erie to Boston."

"You still planning on taking her to Boston?"

He sighed, uncertain of his answer. "I don't know. We'll figure that out as we get closer, and a big part of that decision will be based on what you find out. I'll let you know as soon as I get everything sent to you." Disconnecting, he laid his phone down but remained quiet. Watching the exit signs, he flipped on his blinker and maneuvered down the exit ramp. Finding a small diner with easy parking for the U-Haul, he pulled to a stop.

Twisting around to face her, she did the same, giving her attention to him. "We're going to go in, use their facilities, and get something to eat. But before we go, I need you to get all the information that you have. I'm going to forward it to my contacts so that they can look at it."

Her eyes widened, and she gave a little shake of her head. "Levi, I'm uncomfortable with that. I shouldn't even have this client's records outside the office, and now I'm supposed to share them with people I don't know? What I did was unethical, but I couldn't think of anything else to do. Now it feels even more unethical."

"Claire, I don't think you get this. Mark Martins is not a man who's going to take losing this money easily. By putting that money into your account, he thought he had you under his thumb. Instead, you took off. If he can't get it back from you, then he's going to have to take it from his own account to repay the client. On top of that, I can assure you, he does not want to go to jail. We got away from whoever he sent after you for now, but we need to figure out what Martins is doing. If he hasn't already, he's going to figure out a way to pin this on you and then call the authorities."

He heard her sharp intake of breath, and, despite his vow to keep this professional, he reached across the console and took her hand in his, hoping to infuse some of his warmth into her frozen fingers. "Trust me."

She held his gaze and nodded slowly. Gently pulling her hand away from his, she unbuckled and leaned toward the back seat. Lifting a nondescript bag from her belongings, she pulled out her laptop and said, "Everything's on here."

"Show me."

She opened her laptop and typed in a password, and soon, he saw the files where she had all the records stored. "Attach everything you've got into an email." Once she had done this, he slid the laptop onto the console and typed in the secure address given to him by

LSI. Hitting send, he picked up his phone and waited a few seconds. Soon the text came in.

Secured. Looks good. Working on it now.

Turning back to Claire, he said, "Okay, this is all we can do right now. But while we're here, we need to keep our eyes open, watch our backs, and stick together. We'll hit the restrooms first." Gaining her nod, he climbed out of the SUV and met her at the front. They walked in and headed to the restrooms. It didn't take him long and he was outside the ladies' room door when she walked through. With his hand now resting on her lower back, he escorted her to the front where the hostess then showed them to a booth. He looked around but could perceive no threat. It was almost midday, but the scent of coffee and the all-day breakfast menu called to him.

"I'm desperate for coffee, eggs, and bacon," Claire mumbled.

He chuckled, realizing that the breakfast menu was calling to her as well. With everything they'd gone through, it felt good to smile, even if for just a moment.

It did not take long for their food to be served and their coffee to be refilled. He looked across the table and watched as Claire picked at her food, eating small bites. "You need to eat."

"I know," she agreed. "But it's as though the food gets stuck in my throat."

"That's tension and nerves." Sighing, he nodded toward her plate. "The scrambled eggs are soft. Try getting those down. Then see if you can eat the bacon.

At least the protein will help you feel better. We can take the toast with us."

She nodded and began to focus on the eggs, eating most of them. Their conversation was nonexistent, neither seeming to know what to say. Finally, she leaned back and pushed her plate away. He felt her eyes on him and, as he sipped his coffee, held her steady gaze. "We might as well address the elephant in the room."

She obviously knew what he was talking about when she nodded. "Okay. When you showed up in my room this morning and took care of…. him… you were immediately pissed at me and wanted me to start talking. That's the attitude of someone who came with an agenda."

She cut to the chase, and he inwardly admired that trait. Considering how much to tell her, he said, "I told you that my new job is with a security company. I called one of my coworkers last night and asked about you."

Her chin jerked inward and she lifted an eyebrow, showing surprise. "Why?"

"Because you were traveling with me. Because I knew nothing about you—"

"You knew nothing about me?" She huffed. "What about our conversation yesterday? What about our conversation last night over dinner?"

"Claire, that was two people getting to know each other, but, unlike meeting through friends, I knew nothing about you. I had just offered to take you all the way to Boston, spending almost two days in the car together. Yes, I enjoyed your company but felt like I needed to know more about you."

She was quiet for a moment, and he could have sworn hurt passed through her eyes before she lowered them and focused on the napkin she was shredding in her hand.

Nodding slowly, she said, "Okay, I can accept that. So, what did you find out?"

He hesitated, no longer certain how much he wanted to tell her. *She's been through so much, and now it feels like I'm piling more on her.* Her gaze was still steady, waiting for his answer. He scrubbed his hand over his chin, hating to go into the details. "All I found out was that you had left your job under a cloud. That came from an internal email from Mark Martins about suspicions of embezzlement. That information made me nervous and gave me concerns about taking you all the way to Boston."

"So, you laid awake last night thinking about how you were going to dump me on the side of the road."

He leaned forward, irritation filling him. "I wasn't going to dump you on the side of the road, Claire. But yes, I was going to make sure that you were okay and then allow you to go back to your original decision to get a rental car to take you where you wanted to go."

"What made you come to my room this morning?"

"You weren't in the lobby and, well… I just wanted to get it over with."

She looked back down at her hands and the now-shredded napkin and didn't say anything.

"Claire." As he called her name, she lifted her chin and stared at him, so he continued, "As soon as you told me your story, I believed you."

A snort erupted and she shook her head. "I think it's a little bit more than that, Levi. You still had your people check on me and find out what I told you was true. That's hardly trust." He started to speak but her hand snapped up to stop him. "You know what, I get it. I really do. You stopped by the side of the road to help me and didn't expect any of this to happen. Honestly, I don't blame you for being suspicious. In this day and age, no one can be too careful. I, more than anyone, should know that."

They fell into silence for a moment, each lost in their own thoughts. "Let's hit the bathroom again before we get on the road. There's a gas station next door and we can fill up and then be on our way." She hesitated, but he pressed on, "Please. I know you're upset and angry, but please, don't make a poor decision and say you're going to stay here. You're safer with me."

She opened her mouth and then snapped it closed, grimacing as she seemed to struggle with what to say. Her shoulders slumped and she sighed. "I know this sounds ridiculous because we just met yesterday, but it almost felt like fate. Especially by the time we'd gotten to know each other over dinner, it seemed... well, it seemed really nice." Giving her head a little shake, she added in a stronger voice, "Right. I don't have a lot of choices, so I'll stick with you for now." With that, she slid out of the booth and headed to the ladies' room, leaving him sitting alone, staring at her back.

7

Claire was exhausted but could only imagine that Levi was more so. After eating, they got back onto the road, taking a northern route on the highway past Lake Erie to Buffalo, and then east to Syracuse, only stopping for gas and snacks. She had no idea how long they were going to drive. For that matter, she had no idea what to tell him when they reached Boston.

As though reading her mind, he suddenly asked, "Why Boston?"

Hating to sound impetuous or stupid, she sighed. "I had a roommate who was from Boston. She came to Chicago for college and then went back."

"Is she expecting you?"

She shook her head. "No, not really. We're friends, but not exactly close friends. We chat a couple of times a year... mostly birthdays and Christmas. I sent her a text the morning I left out, but she didn't reply right away. Truthfully? I couldn't think of anywhere else to go. She finally replied last night and told me that she was traveling for her job and was out of the country. She did say that I was more than welcome to stay in her condo and that if I wanted to accept, just let her know and she'd make sure the doorman gave me a key."

Levi was quiet and she snuck a look toward him, seeing his jaw tight. Tired and frustrated, she bit out, "Look, I know it wasn't a great plan, but I didn't know what else to do. I was terrified of staying in Chicago. The idea that the police would come banging on my door and arrest me for embezzlement had me running away. Yes, I have a couple of good friends, but I don't want to put them in danger either."

"Claire, it's okay. I'm just glad you got away."

She felt deflated and blinked away the sting of tears. "I can go to her place in Boston and hide out for a while. But beyond that, I have no plan."

"Look, hopefully tonight, we'll know more from my coworkers about what's going on. Once everything is taken care of and you're safe, you can decide where you want to go."

She grabbed a tissue from her purse and wiped her nose, sniffling softly. "Yeah, you're right. It's just weird. If the head of the company is involved in something illegal, then I technically have no job to go back to. I have no family in Chicago anymore, and even though I have some friends, maybe now is the time to make the great leap to change." She looked over at him and offered a little smile. "Kind of like you."

He chuckled and nodded, and she loved hearing that sound. The day had been so tense that seeing him smile made everything seem a little brighter. Tired of talking, she asked, "What kind of music do you like to listen to?"

"My taste in music is eclectic. I have to admit since my last couple of years have been in Wyoming, I listen to a lot of country. But honestly, my favorite would be jazz."

She flipped on the sound system and quickly found a light jazz station. "How's that?"

He looked toward her, his gaze searing straight into her, and said, "It's perfect. Absolutely perfect." For a few seconds, she wondered if he was only talking about the music. Blushing, she looked away. Closing her eyes, she pushed all thoughts of the handsome man being anything more than her rescuer out of her mind and allowed the soft music to lull her to sleep.

Levi was glad that Claire was finally able to take a nap. Dealing with the multiple emotions during the day, he could only imagine how much worse it was for her. With all that they had discussed, they hadn't talked about the near abduction that morning. Fairly certain she'd never had a gun held on her before, he assumed she was burying that fear down deep.

Glancing at the GPS and the clock, he maneuvered down the exit ramp near Albany. A plan had begun to form, but he needed some time to think about it before discussing it with her. If her heart was still set on going to Boston, he would take her there. If she was no longer certain that was where she wanted to go, they had a decision to make.

Finding a hotel with an uncrowded parking lot, he pulled into a space with room for the trailer, and she roused awake.

"Oh, my gosh! How long did I sleep?"

"Don't worry, Claire. You were only out for about thirty minutes."

"Where are we?"

"Albany."

She looked out the window toward the hotel and inhaled sharply. He glanced her way and watched her pale, much like how she had that morning. *Shit, I didn't even think about what it would be like for her to be in another hotel.*

She jerked her head around, her eyes wide. "I don't think I can do this—"

"We'll share a room." The words had burst forth unexpectedly, but he knew it was the only way either of them would get any rest. He would be assured she was protected, and she would be able to relax. She sucked in her lips and stared, not speaking.

"Look, we can get a room with two beds, and that way, we can both sleep. I'll be there for protection, and we'll be able to rest easy by not having to worry about you. I promise it'll be fine. Just sleep."

As though realizing what he was assuring, she shook her head back and forth quickly, her hair swinging about her face. "Don't worry about that, Levi! I'm not concerned about sharing a room with you. In fact, you're right, it's the only way I'll be able to relax."

With that settled, they climbed from the SUV, both stretching the kinks out, and walked into the lobby together. He again requested a room on the first floor, close to where he could keep an eye on his SUV and U-Haul. Taking care of the accommodations, he grabbed the room key and they moved the SUV closer.

Inserting the key card, he threw open the door but noticed her feet did not move forward. Reaching back, he linked fingers with her and gently guided her forward. She clung to his hand as they entered the basic hotel room. He locked the door behind them and, without her needing to ask, they searched the room together. Bathroom, consisting of a toilet, sink with a long counter, and tub/shower combination. Closet filled with nothing but an iron and coat hangers. They even looked under the two queen beds covered with tacky, flowered bedspreads. Once she was assured that there was no one there but them, she audibly sighed.

A local pizzeria flyer was on the desk, and, after checking her preferences, he called in an order. "I hope that's okay. I just figured it would be easier if we stayed here."

Nodding, she smiled. "I don't know how you do it, Levi, but it's as though you're reading my mind. I'm so tired but also hungry. And you're right, I don't want to go out anywhere."

"You're safe here. They probably traced you to the previous hotel because of your debit card. But what that also tells us is that he has a reach."

She scrunched her nose and shook her head. "A reach?"

"Someone beyond just a man who's embezzling from his company. If I had to guess, he's probably involved in organized crime. That's probably how he had a go-to man like the one who showed up this morning. But now, we've got you off the radar."

She nodded while listening, then yawned.

"Why don't you go take a shower and relax. I'm going to see what my coworkers can tell me, and the pizza should be here when you get out." She gathered her toiletries and he watched as she walked into the bathroom. As soon as he heard the water running, he called Tate.

"Hey, man. Where are you?"

"Albany."

"How's it going?"

"It's fine. We've had a chance to talk, and I think she trusts me. I have to confess, I'm glad we're able to help her." He heard a chuckle and rolled his eyes. "Okay, okay, that's all this is… me playing rescuer. Don't make it into more."

Tate was still chuckling, but said, "Okay, here's what we've been able to discern. Mark Martins is definitely tied in to some of the illegal betting that goes on in Chicago. It doesn't seem as though he's connected to just one particular mob family, but it appears he has several of them as clients. And from what Josh can tell, if he's been as creative with his other clients as he was with the one that Claire discovered, he's moving money, laundering money, and embezzling a ton. The five hundred thousand dollars she noticed isn't much overall, but he doesn't want to be caught. He could have easily traced her through the debit card she used at the motel... it was tied into the bank that he used to make the transfer into her account. You can tell her not to panic. We disabled that card."

"Good. Thanks, Tate. I don't how to repay you for this. It's certainly not how I expected to come into the job."

"Is she still going to Boston? If so, it's going to make it harder to try to protect her there. But we can turn all this over to the FBI."

"I found out she only had a college roommate that lived in Boston but isn't there right now. Claire can stay at the condo, she's got nothing there. No job. No friends. No family."

"Doesn't sound like Boston's the answer."

"Yeah, I thought the same thing. I just don't know what is." Levi sighed, dragging his hand through his hair.

"Well, if she's got nowhere else to go, what about here?"

Levi jolted, sitting up straighter. Uncertain he heard Tate correctly, he asked, "There?"

"Look, I'm not trying to make things complicated for you, but it sounds like you really like this woman."

Shaking his head even though Tate obviously couldn't see him, he said, "Are you seriously suggesting I bring someone I practically just met to Maine with me?"

"You don't understand what it's like around here. I'm the only one who got with my old high school girlfriend. Hell, the other Keepers are with people they met on missions."

"Yeah, and I remember me telling you that I liked things uncomplicated."

Tate's chuckle now turned into laughter. "Uncomplicated? That's the same as boring, man."

Levi had no response to that, so he remained quiet, his mind racing.

"Whatever you decide, just let us know. Get some rest, and we'll talk to you in the morning. Just keep in mind that she's welcome to come here. As far as Mace is concerned, this is a mission."

He disconnected, heard the water turn off in the bathroom, and a knock sounded on the door. Checking the security hole, he opened the door and paid for the pizza. Locking the door again, he turned around and watched Claire walk out of the bathroom. Fresh. Clean. And smiling. Absolutely beautiful. *Fuckin' hell. There's no denying it... things are definitely complicated.*

8

While in the shower, Claire had attempted to steer her mind away from the handsome man who had swooped into her world. *I need to focus on what's going on with me and what on earth I'm going to do about my job and my life.* By the time she'd used the hotel toiletries and scrubbed her hair and body, she forced her thoughts to what was next.

She hated to stay in her friend's condo alone but, not having another choice, hoped she would be safe there. If Levi's contacts could offer advice as to who she could trust and turn to, she could get the information over to the authorities. She had no doubt she would still have to go back to Chicago at some time, *but on my terms with the authorities on my side and not with them escorting me back in handcuffs!*

Once clean, she threw on a slouchy shirt over a sports bra and leggings. After moisturizing, she ran a comb through her long hair, sweeping it away from her face. Her hand hesitated on the doorknob before entering the hotel room, the fear from this morning's attack still fresh on her mind. Hearing Levi's voice in the room and the tantalizing scent of pizza brought her back to the present. Throwing open the door, she stepped out.

The sight of him standing in the room, dark stubble casting a shadow over his face, she could still feel the intensity of his gaze as it raked over her. Suddenly, she rethought the idea of spending the night in the same room, albeit in different beds. *No, it'll be fine. He sees me as a woman to protect.* The idea that he might need protection from her almost caused an exhausted giggle to slip out, but she managed to cough into her hand instead.

Her gaze dropped from his hair that appeared to have had his hand dragged through it, down his muscular body, to his bare feet. *Shit, even his feet are sexy.* Her gaze made its way back up again. His eyes remained steady on her although his mouth opened several times without saying anything.

He finally jolted and lifted the box in his hand. "Pizza's here."

Her lips curved into a smile and she nodded. "I can see that. I can also smell it!"

She walked toward him and lifted the lid on the box, the pizza still steaming hot and the scent even more tantalizing. The hotel room was not large, and since they had no plates, she waved toward one of the beds. "We can set it in between us and just eat here."

While she handled the pizza, he popped the top on the water bottles. She sat cross-legged on top of the bed and reached for a slice. Not waiting, she bit off the thick, chewy bite, the cheese stretching between the slice and her lips. She closed her eyes and groaned in ecstasy, moaning, "Oh, my God! That's amazing!"

As she finished chewing and swallowing, she opened her eyes and looked up at Levi reclining against the pillows, his slice of pizza halted on his way to his mouth as he stared slack-jawed at her. Her free hand shot to her mouth, wondering if she had pizza sauce or cheese on her face. Her fingers encountered no mess, and just as she was about to ask if he was all right, he blinked out of his apparent trance and shoved a big bite of pizza into his mouth. Assuming he was just as tired as she, they continued eating in silence for several minutes.

He was so quiet while they ate, she wondered if he regretted his offer to share a room. "Listen, Levi, I feel like we need to be honest. If this is uncomfortable for you... being here with me, I get it. If you'd rather have your own room—"

"No, I'm good. Unless you'd rather me make other arrangements—"

"No, I'm good, too."

Silence descended again, and this time she was unable to hold back a giggle. His eyes widened as they sought hers, and she shook her head. "I'm sorry. It's not that anything about our situation is funny. I suppose I'm just tired and a stupid giggle was the only thing that made its way out of my mouth."

A smile spread across his face and he nodded. "It's okay, Claire. Go ahead and laugh or giggle or cry or scream—well, probably don't scream. If you did, someone might call the cops."

She laughed. "I promise I won't scream unless we have another morning like this morning." Suddenly her mirth fled, and she sucked in a quick breath.

He leaned forward and placed his hands over hers. "My promise to you is that we won't have a morning like we did today."

She bit her bottom lip and nodded, his words soothing over her, providing comfort as well as the touch of his hands on hers offering a steady force. She turned her hands over and clasped his, holding on. Warmth settled over her, emanating from their touch. Lifting her gaze, she found his eyes pinned on her, his emotions unfathomable. Swallowing deeply, she leaned forward slightly, closing the gap between them.

Suddenly, he let go of her hands and leaned back, and she immediately felt the cold at their missed connection. He stood, grabbed the now-empty box, and dumped it into the trash can. She escaped into the bathroom, needing a moment away from his presence. After brushing her teeth, she stared into the mirror and shook her head. *Don't be stupid. He's a good guy. He's here out of a sense of duty and responsibility. Not because he's infatuated with me!* Regaining her courage, she stepped out of the bathroom.

His bag was on the second bed. Inclining his head toward the bed closest to her, he said, "You take that one. I'll sleep closer to the door."

His statement made sense and she nodded. He went into the bathroom, and she slid under the covers, wondering if she would ever find sleep. But fatigue dragged her under because that was the last thought she had before she drifted away.

Walking out of the bathroom several minutes later, the illumination from behind him cast a glow over the beds. Moving closer, Levi could see that Claire was already asleep. He usually slept in just boxers but wanted to be prepared while not making her uncomfortable, so he chose drawstring sweatpants. Moving to the other bed, he climbed under the covers and plumped the pillows. Years of training gave him the ability to sleep while still maintaining a watchful eye. Having made sure the room was secure before he'd gone into the bathroom, he closed his eyes.

An hour later, the sound of whimpering woke him. Jerking, he looked over and saw Claire moving restlessly in her bed, fearful sounds coming from her. Tossing back the covers, he stood and leaned over her bed. She appeared asleep but fitful. Touching her shoulder gently, he whispered, "Claire, it's all right." Her eyes snapped open and she reached out, grabbing his hand. Uncertain if she was awake or still in a semiconscious state, her grasp continued to hold his tightly. He stroked her hair away from her face and murmured gentle sounds.

"Don't leave me," her tortured voice whispered in return. "Please, don't leave me."

She closed her eyes but the death grip on his hand

remained firm. Lifting the covers, he slid into bed next to her and wrapped his arms around her shaking body. She immediately stilled, her breaths slowing and becoming more even.

He lay for several minutes with the idea of only holding her until she fell into a deep slumber again. The scent of her shampoo wafted over him, and even though it was the same one he had used from the hotel, on her it seemed much sweeter. Her skin was soft, and her body began to warm with his wrapped around her. He tried to ignore the feel of her curves, focusing on keeping her safe from her own dreams. *I'll just lay here for a few more minutes until she's calm and goes back to sleep.*

Many hours later, he woke from a restful sleep, instantly aware of two things. One, he was not alone. The other was that his morning wood was nestled tightly against the soft stomach of the woman whose eyes were open and pinned on his.

He knew he should shift backward. He knew he should apologize. He knew he should make a joke about not being able to control his baser instincts around a beautiful woman in hopes that she would laugh in return. But with her dark eyes holding his gaze, her breath coming out in little puffs dancing across his face, and her arms wrapped tightly around him, he didn't do what he knew he should.

Before he had a chance to move away, she made the decision for both of them. Leaning forward, she pressed her lips against his. Over the last two days, he'd wondered what it would be like to kiss her, but his imaginings had not prepared him for reality. A jolt of electricity ripped through his body and his arms tightened about her. Angling his head, they both moved as one, taking the kiss deeper, wilder, and sweeter.

She pressed her body closer and it took every ounce of self-control he had to keep from sliding her panties down her legs and plunging himself into her warm sex. Against every fiber of his being crying out for release, he pulled back. He saw the questioning move through her eyes and rushed to explain. "I'm not denying you, Claire. I'm not denying this. I just can't take advantage of you."

"What if it's what I want?"

Her soft voice wrapped around him, and he struggled for self-control. "You've got to believe it's what I want, too, but we have a lot to figure out. A lot to talk about this morning. And, as much as I want your sweet body, I want to make sure you're taken care of." He held his breath, hoping his words made sense and that she wouldn't push him away in a huff, pissed and insulted.

She continued to hold his gaze for a long moment before her lips curved slightly. "You really are a good guy, aren't you? You really are the best." She leaned forward and placed a soft kiss on the corner of his mouth, then sat up in bed.

Her hair was adorably messy, and with her slouchy shirt hanging off one shoulder that begged to be kissed, it was easy to imagine waking up to this woman every day. *But I have nothing to offer her... not even a place to stay.* Sighing, he leaned forward and placed his hand behind her head and pulled her toward him, kissing her once more before she left the bed to get ready for the day.

Moving faster than he imagined she could, she threw her leg over his thighs, straddled his lap, and pressed close, mumbling against his lips. "No promises… no regrets. Just you and me… right here, right now."

9

As soon as she kissed him, she knew she wanted more. More of his taste, more kisses, more of him. Always cautious and careful until recently, she was ready to toss her cares away just to have this moment with Levi.

Straddling his hips, her core rubbed against his erection as she tried to ease the all-consuming need for friction. She felt each one of his fingertips as they dug into her ass, and her breasts crushed against his chest. Once again, she kissed him, their tongues tangling.

His groin surged upward, and she moaned at the feel of his length. Suddenly, her clothes were too constricting and, with her hands planted on his chest, she pushed upward. Grabbing the hem of her slouchy shirt, she jerked it over her head and tossed it toward the back of the bed. Her sports bra was functional but not sexy—and not easy to get off. She squiggled and wiggled out of it and tossed it to the side as well.

She grinned as she watched his face, his eyes darkening as his gaze landed on her breasts as they bounced with her movements. His hands, which had held her hips, glided upward and now palmed their weight as his thumbs circled her nipples.

The electricity rushed over her, crackling along her nerves between her breasts and her core. She dropped her head back, closing her eyes, giving in completely to the sensations jolting through her body. They were still mostly dressed, and yet this was the most erotic she had ever felt with any partner.

Leaning forward, she shifted upward so that her nipples dangled as a tantalizing gift in front of his face. Answering her silent beckoning, he pulled one deep into his mouth as his fingers rolled the other. Barely aware of her movements, she rubbed her hips back and forth, dragging along the length of his cock.

If she had been paying attention, she might've been prepared for his movements, but instead, she blinked in surprise as he suddenly lifted her, flipping her onto her back as he leapt from the bed. *No! Oh, no!*

Her eyes watched in anguish as he stalked away, but he only walked to his bag. Reaching inside, he pulled out a condom, holding it between his thumb and forefinger as he turned back toward the bed. His dark gaze held hers, and air rushed from her lungs in relief as her smile met his intense stare. With her thumbs hooked into her waistband, she shucked her leggings and panties downward, kicking them off her feet. He was doing the same thing with his sweatpants, and for the first time, she was able to admire all of Levi.

His muscular shoulders and chest had been evident this morning when she awoke, but now, seeing his naked thighs, muscular ass, and impressive cock, she could barely catch her breath with his beautiful masculinity on display. He stood by the side of the bed, not moving, his gaze never leaving her face. For a moment, she didn't understand his hesitation. Then it hit her. *He really is a good guy.*

She nodded and said, "Yes. I want this. I want you."

Now it was his turn to move quickly. After rolling on the condom, he crawled over her body, his mouth latching onto hers. They kissed, tongues tangling, before he licked his way over her jaw, down her neck, then circling her nipple.

She could care less that she'd only known this man for two days. She could care less that she was taking everything he was offering on faith. Right now, her body cried out for him and her heart trusted him.

As his mouth left her breasts, he continued kissing his way down her stomach until his shoulders shifted between her thighs. Now, his mouth latched onto her slick folds, licking and sucking. Inserting a long finger into her sex while he sucked on her clit, she panted as the inner coil tightened. Her short nails scraped along his scalp as she lifted her hips, trying to erase the minuscule space between them. Crying out through gritted teeth, her release rushed over her as her body shattered.

Dragging in oxygen in an attempt to clear her vision, she watched a slow grin spread over his face and knew that no matter what else ever happened in her life, she would remember that one perfect moment.

Licking and kissing his way back up her body, he

nestled his cock between her thighs. Her hands now clutched his back, her fingertips digging in slightly. Once again, he hesitated and she begged, "Please."

With a single thrust, he plunged balls deep and she gasped at the fullness. They began moving as one, and she met each thrust. Soon, the friction had her racing toward the finish line, desperately wanting to fly across it with him. She wrapped her legs around his waist, digging her heels into his muscular ass. His hand moved between their bodies, and he lightly pinched her clit. As he thrust over and over, she shattered once again and he quickly followed, tensing, groaning out his own release.

For long moments they lay, limbs tangled, breaths mingled, heartbeats pounding in unison. As consciousness slowly came over them, she reached up and cupped his jaw, smoothing her thumb over the lines emanating from his eyes. She leaned forward and kissed him lightly, murmuring against his lips. "Thank you. For everything... just thank you."

His hand cupped her face as well, and his breath rushed warm over her cheeks. "No need to thank me, Claire, because this has absolutely been my pleasure."

She kept the smile on her face, but her heart twinged. She had told him she didn't expect anything but now recognized what her heart knew but her brain had refused to see. She wanted this man. This really good man.

Once breakfast was consumed, Levi and Claire were

back in the SUV and on the highway heading east toward Boston. He wondered if their morning would be filled with awkward, post-sex attempts at conversation, but, as usual with her, he smiled as they had no problem finding things to talk about. Glancing to the side, he memorized her profile, watching as she tucked her hair behind her ear.

With no delays, they would arrive in Boston in about three hours. *Three hours to find out what she's doing, what she wants, and what she needs.* He hadn't planned on sleeping with her but couldn't deny that she'd not only rocked his body but rocked his world… and he didn't want to let her go. *How can someone fall so hard so fast?* His mind wanted to deny that was what had happened, but the ache in his chest at the thought of her leaving told him how much he wanted to be with her.

Wishing he had the finesse to ease into the conversation, he simply blurted, "So, what are you going to do in Boston?" Her sigh was audible, filled with heaviness, and he glanced to the side as she shook her head slowly.

"I don't know." Still shaking her head, she continued, "Unlike you, who had time to plan the next phase of your life, I haven't had that. Honestly? I never even considered that I would be in danger, other than being afraid the police would show up at my door. I don't even know what to do about it all."

"My people can turn what they had found out over to the FBI."

"That makes sense, but what do you think?" She shifted around to look at him.

Looking to the side again, he saw her earnest

expression focused on him, and he longed to gently rub the crease between her brows. "I agree, it makes sense. If you don't, you'll always be looking over your shoulder to see if Mark Martins is sending someone else after you." He watched her visibly shudder and reached over to place his hand on hers.

They were silent for several moments, their fingers still linked, and she seemed to be struggling with her thoughts. Finally, she said, "I know that I'm lucky to have met you. I mean, what are the odds of meeting someone who has your connections and your past in law enforcement? We definitely need to let the FBI know, and I'd rather be on the offense telling what happened than be on the defense trying to convince someone I didn't steal the money."

He released a breath he hadn't realized he was holding and reluctantly let go of her hand to grab his phone. Pressing a button, he connected. "She agrees. Send it all to the agent I told you about."

"Copy that. Keep us informed and let us know if you need help."

He disconnected and felt her eyes pinned on him again.

"That's amazing that all you have to do is make a phone call and someone on the other end makes it all better."

He laughed and nodded. "What's even crazier is that I haven't had my official first day as their employee yet."

Her laughter rang out, and he loved the sound, glad to see her smile and the tension lines in her face and the tightness in her shoulders relax.

"Are you going to be okay in Boston all by yourself?"

She sobered, shrugging. "I have no idea. I don't know if I can get a job in my field as long as this mess is hanging over my head. I'm sure I'll have to be interviewed by the FBI, and I don't know how long I'll be able to stay in my friend's condo." She lifted her hands and threaded her fingers through her hair, pulling it away from her face as she squeezed her eyes tightly shut. Finally, snorting, she shook her head. "I'm not terribly interested in Boston; I just chose it because I had no idea where else to go."

"Do you want to go back to Chicago? Once everything is settled and it's safe?"

Shifting in her seat to face him, she replied with a question of her own. "What made you decide to leave Wyoming and the FBI?"

Shocked at the change in topics, he thought for a moment. "It wasn't any one particular thing. Wyoming was fine, but I can't say I had any good friends there. I often worked alone, and it seemed as though my job had become more administrative than anything else. I had the opportunity to work with a man that I became friends with. He was back in Wyoming visiting family, but when he'd gotten out of the military, he started working for a security company. Getting to know him and talking to him, I became interested. You're right, I took my time. I thought of the pros and cons. But more and more, the pros outweighed the cons, and I decided to make the career change." He glanced at her, once more finding her focus completely on him.

She nodded her agreement. "I get that, Levi. I really

do. I suppose it seems that everything I did was completely impetuous... and, in truth, it was. But part of me had been longing for a change. Martins and Lee Investment Company was never going to be where I spent my whole career. They were a little too *'old boy network'* for me, and I knew I'd never advance there. I actually liked the bank job I had before that, even though it didn't pay as much."

She continued to think in silence for a few more moments and then added, "Outside Chicago is where I was born and raised, but with my parents no longer there and quite a few of my friends having left, I didn't enjoy the city as much as I had when I was younger. I guess perhaps I'd been looking for a reason to make a change and what happened simply forced the issue."

"So, I'll repeat my question... is Boston where you really want to go?"

Once more the silence filled the cab, and he glanced at the highway sign, pulling off at a rest stop. Putting the SUV in park, he unbuckled and turned in his seat, facing her. She glanced outside at their surroundings, then turned back to him in question.

She shook her head and sighed. "No, not really. I just don't have a backup plan right now."

He reached across the console and took her hand, wanting the physical connection while battling the desire to pull her closer. "So, what *do* you know?"

She looked down at their linked fingers and then back up to his face. "I know that I need a place to regroup. I know that I need to feel safe. I know I've stood on my own for a long time, but in two days I've discovered how nice it is to have someone to help." She pinched her lips together and sucked in a breath through her nose before letting it out slowly. "And, if we're sticking to honesty, I know that I can't imagine saying goodbye to you."

The air left his lungs in a rush, and he reached with his free hand to grab the back of her head and bring her forward, their lips meeting. Firm met soft as their mouths melded together. She opened her lips in a little sigh, and he slid his tongue into her warmth, the jolt of lust shooting through him as her tongue moved over his.

Leaning back, barely able to catch his breath from a kiss that reminded him what they'd shared this morning, he held her gaze. "We're at a crossroads, Claire."

Her brow furrowed as she continued to cling to his shoulders. "What crossroads is that?"

He nodded to the right and said, "That's the way to Boston. You say the word, and that's the road we'll get on. I'll take you wherever you want to go and make sure you're safe before I leave."

Chest heaving, she barely whispered, "And the other choice?"

Nodding straight ahead, he said, "That's the way to Maine. I don't even have a place to live right now. I've got use of a cabin until I find my own place. My job hasn't officially started until I get there. I'm not in a position to make promises other than to say I'll keep you safe and help you as you figure out the next step in your life."

"Why would you do that for me, Levi?"

"Because honestly, Claire, sweetheart, I can't imagine saying goodbye to you, either."

A slow smile spread over her face, her beauty slamming into him, causing his heart to pound even more than it already was. She slowly nodded as her smile widened and her eyes shone brightly. "Then what are we waiting for? Let's go to Maine."

10

They stopped for gas on the north side of Boston, having taken the interstate that circled widely around the city. While Levi pumped gas, Claire ran into the ladies' room. Grabbing a few snacks, she pulled out her wallet, remembering to use her credit card and not her now-disabled debit card.

His eyes landed on her as she walked back to the SUV and his smile warmed her heart, giving her hope that better days were coming. Unable to stop, she leaned forward and placed her hands on either side of his jaws. Without hesitation, she kissed him, loving the feel of his firm lips underneath hers. They opened their mouths at the same time, their tongues immediately seeking entrance, tangling and dancing together.

He tasted of coffee and cinnamon and she wanted more. Much more. Now that she knew what lay under his clothes—especially behind the zipper of his jeans—she hoped she'd have the opportunity for more.

His hands moved over her back, skimming down to

her waist where his fingertips flexed, pressing in before gliding upward. She felt his thumb sweeping underneath her breast and wished they were no longer in his SUV in the middle of the parking lot.

He finally dragged his mouth away but kept his forehead pressed against hers, his breath ragged. "What are you thinking?"

"Honestly? I wish we were somewhere private and not in the middle of the parking lot so that I could keep kissing you the way I want."

He laughed and lifted his head, now pressing his lips against her forehead. "Me too."

"How much longer do we have to go?"

"This exit is right at the Massachusetts and Maine state lines. According to GPS, we should be at our destination in less than three hours." Almost on cue, his phone sent an alert indicating an accident ahead on the highway, causing delays. They looked at each other and he smiled. "It might take a little longer, but how about we take some back roads?"

Laughing, she nodded. "Two days ago, I thought getting stuck off the highway was the worst! But now, I think maybe the best adventures are found on back roads."

Grinning, he kissed her lightly before starting the SUV, and she watched as he passed by the entrance ramp to get onto the highway and they started along the coast road north into Maine.

The scenery was gorgeous, and she said, "Growing up in the city, I became so used to skyscrapers and concrete. But this takes my breath away."

"I know what you mean. Granted, the scenery in Wyoming was amazing as well. But these forests that run right to the edge of the ocean are pretty spectacular."

"What's gonna happen when you get to Maine? I mean, if you'd never met me, how was that going to work?"

"The company I work for has a small cabin near their base, and they said I can use it while I'm looking for a place to live. I looked at it when I came to interview for the job and met everyone. It's small but nice. The boss actually let his now-wife and son use it when she needed a place to get away. In fact, I think two of the other wives may have used it as well."

She grew quiet, nibbling on her bottom lip as she wondered about the future. She wished she had a little more time with him before they arrived. "Are they expecting you today?" She felt his stare but dreaded to see his questioning gaze, so she continued to face forward.

"No, not really. Originally, I told them that I was going to take a whole week to get from Wyoming to Maine. Why?"

"Oh... I don't know..."

"Hey, you always say the word *honesty*. In just two days, I already associate that with you. So, just say what you're thinking."

Licking her lips, she glanced to the side, seeing nothing but interest in his eyes. And maybe a touch of lust as well. *God, I hope so!* "It's just weird. They're expecting *you*... not you bringing some stray."

"Claire, you are not some stray!"

"I know you said your boss considered this to be a mission. I don't really even know what that means, but I still doubt they're expecting you to bring your *mission* along with you."

"When I came to interview for the job, I had a chance to meet the others. Except for my friend Tate, the other men that are in relationships all met their women when on a mission."

She blinked, her chin jerking in slightly. "You're kidding?"

Shaking his head, he said, "Nope. From what they tell me, it takes a special woman to be able to have a relationship with someone who's in security."

Uncertainty still ate at her. "Well, when we get there, should I find a hotel?"

"If that's what you want."

"What other choice do I have?"

"Stay with me. At the cabin."

The air rushed from her lungs, and she held his gaze, seeing a twinkle in his eyes. "Levi, what exactly are you saying?"

"I'd like you to stay with me, at least until we figure out what we want. We can eat. Rest. Whatever."

Brows lifted at his suggestion, she grinned. "Whatever?"

"If I'm being honest, too, Claire, I'd like to keep kissing you as well. It's the *whatever* I'm really looking forward to."

Sucking in a quick breath, her smile widened. "Then

LEVI

I'm all in. I'll stay at the cabin with you until I figure out my next step. And we can... whatever."

Levi grabbed his phone and called Tate. "Just wanted to let you know that we should be there early this afternoon."

"It'll be good to finally have you here, man. I'm glad you gave me a heads up. The women have gone into planning mode."

"Planning mode?"

"I told Nora that you might bring someone and gave her an explanation of what was happening."

"How did you know? I didn't until just now!"

Tate laughed and said, "I told you not to fight it. Mace and Drew's wives were already planning for Claire's arrival with you since they work here and know the whole story, but Nora let the others know. They're planning to welcome Claire with open arms."

Levi hated for anyone to go to trouble, but it warmed his heart to know the other Keepers' women would make Claire feel welcome.

"Just to let you know, we sent the information to your contact at the Chicago office of the FBI. As you can imagine, he's thrilled. He said they've been taking a look at Mark Martins for a while but didn't have anything concrete. He'll want to talk to Claire soon."

"Sounds good. It still feels strange to have all this working on my behalf, and I haven't even started my employment yet."

"Remember what I said, Levi. As far as we're concerned, you're a Keeper already. Mace considers this to be your first mission with us."

"We both appreciate it. We'll be there soon. We're going to drop my stuff off at the storage unit first." Disconnecting, he looked over at Claire as she beamed her smile his way. "I take it you heard most of that?"

She reached over and gave his hand a squeeze while nodding. "I can't thank you enough for this, Levi." She pulled out her phone and began typing. "I'm letting my friend know that I won't need her condo in Boston... after all, I'm taking the scenic route to Maine." Grinning up at him, she added, "And I can't wait to spend more time with you."

As though she read his mind, he pressed his foot down on the accelerator, anxious to eat up the miles to get to LSI. He had no idea what tomorrow would bring or what decisions Claire would make about her life, but right now, they would stick to the road together.

As the road hugged the rocky coastline, Claire had her nose pressed against the glass. "This is absolutely beautiful!"

Levi grinned, glad to see her so relaxed and enjoying the view. Their speed had slowed on the curvy road considering the trailer towed behind them. Turning his attention back to the drive, he glanced at the extended side mirrors, seeing a car tailgating. Growling, he slowed more on a straight section of road, hoping the car wanted to pass. Instead, the car just slowed as well. "Asshole," he grumbled under his breath.

Suddenly the car pulled into the other lane and sped

up. Looking ahead, Levi cursed, seeing that now there was no room for the other car to pass. "What the fuck is he doing?"

"What's going on?" Claire asked, whipping her head back around to him.

"Some maniac in a car is acting like he's trying to pass but won't actually do it." Driving defensively, he pulled ahead but knew that with the U-Haul trailer, he would never be able to outrun the car. Suddenly, he felt a bump against the trailer, and they swerved, perilously close to the edge of the road.

Claire screamed, and he hit a number on his phone as well as speaker. "Got a tail! Someone's trying to run us off the road! I can't outrun them with the trailer."

"Location?"

"About a mile south from the Coastal Storage Facility."

"Just short of there is a farm. You'll have a bigger area to try to get off the road. We're on our way."

He felt a tap against the trailer again but managed to maintain control of the vehicle. Growling his curses, he looked ahead and saw the lane leading to the farm, extra-wide to allow for tractors and trucks. Cutting the other vehicle off, he turned as carefully as he could while still maintaining speed. The U-Haul trailer lurched to the side, then slammed back down on the gravel lane. A barn was in the distance, and he called out again. "Car still in pursuit. I'm at the farm, heading to the barn."

Looking toward Claire, he said, "I need you to do exactly as I say, babe. Open the glove compartment, pull out my weapon, and lay it on the console. As soon as I stop, you hop out and run into the barn. Get out of sight."

Grateful she followed his directions without question, she nodded and opened the glove compartment. Pulling out his gun, she laid it right where he indicated, within his reach. He sped up, causing the dirt on the lane to swirl into the air all around creating a screen behind them. Suddenly, he jerked to a stop, the barn looming on her side of the vehicle. "Now!"

She hopped out and ducked down as she ran around the front of the SUV, then into the barn. He snatched his gun, threw open his door, and raced after her. He bypassed the door and ran around the far corner of the barn, still hidden by the dust-storm swirling from his tires. The car skidded to a stop behind the U-Haul. Glancing around the corner, he watched Clarence Tolsen, the man that he had disarmed in the hotel, climb out.

The way he'd angled his SUV and trailer, he hoped Clarence had not been able to discern that he had gone in a different direction than Claire. He heard the footsteps approach as they crunched on the gravel and readied his weapon. The steps halted and then retreated. *He's going into the barn. Please, God, let Claire be out of sight!*

Clarence entered through the wide doors of the barn, and Levi soundlessly slipped around the corner. Making his way to the open doors, he could hear Clarence moving inside.

"I know you're up there! I can see the fuckin' straw

move!" Clarence yelled. "You got a choice. You can come down and give me what I want, or I'll burn this fuckin' barn down!"

Levi peeked around the barn door into the cavernous space. The barn was old, and in another time or place, he would have appreciated the architecture. Now, he instantly scanned the interior, seeing bits of straw and dust motes floating through the sunlight streaming through the slats in the wooden walls, but no sign of Claire. *Good girl.*

Staying out of sight, he prepared to take aim when, suddenly, Clarence looked down and yelled. "Shit!" Clarence swung his weapon around and fired at a large snake slithering along the dirt floor. He missed and the snake coiled, raising its head. Clarence fired wildly again at the serpent.

The distraction gave Levi the perfect opportunity to disarm him. Racing forward, he leveled his gun at Clarence's chest and growled, "Drop your weapon."

Clarence's gaze lifted, but he continued to hold onto his weapon. Anger mixed with fear ran through his eyes, then a calculating smirk moved over his face. "It's just you and me, hotshot. Gotta tell you, I don't mind those odds."

Levi had been aware of the sounds of approaching vehicles, and a slow grin spread across his face, now seeing confusion replace the smirk on Clarence's face. "I think my odds just got better." Suddenly, a rush of armed men came in, encircling the two. Glancing to the side, Levi spied Tate. "Good to see you, man."

Tate grinned in return. "You have a good trip?"

"There were a few hiccups." He nodded toward Clarence who now had his gun stripped from him by Walker, one of the other Keepers.

"You certainly know how to make an entrance."

The deep voice coming from behind had him swing around. Looking toward Mace, his new boss, he said, "Normally, I like things uncomplicated." Lifting his gaze up toward the loft, he spied Claire's face peeking down over bales of hay. Her eyes were wide but her smile beamed. As he continued to stare upward, he said, "But now, I think complications and back roads just lead to adventures."

11

Levi accepted another beer from Horace, the older man and former SEAL that Mace hired to help with maintenance around the LSI property. Horace's wife, Marge, a former CIA Special Operator, also helped run the place. She had organized the spread now laid out in front of them, tables groaning with food.

He looked around and was just as stunned as the first time he'd viewed this place. The lighthouse loomed over them, stately and magnificent. The waves crashed on the rocks below where the caves housed much of the heart of LSI.

Shouts and cheers snagged his attention, seeing Josh, Walker, Rank, and Drew locked in a death battle of cornhole.

Hearing laughter, he shifted his gaze toward Claire, surrounded by the other women. Her head was thrown back, a hearty laugh resounding. Her glossy hair hung in waves and her cheeks were now brightened with a natural blush. *God, she's beautiful.* As soon as they arrived at the compound, she was enveloped by the women all checking on her.

Now, in the middle of someone's retelling of their rescue story, she glanced toward him, her smile now beaming just for him. The sunlight danced across her face and she ducked her chin, tucking a wayward strand of hair behind her ear before turning her attention back to the women.

"How're you doing?"

He looked up as several of the Keepers sat in the lawn chairs circling the firepit. Mace, Clay, Josh, Bray, Blake, and Tate settled with their beers as well.

"It was a crazy-ass trip to get here, but..." he glanced back at Claire and finished, "I'm good."

"Hell, y'all are nuts," Clay said, shaking his head. "No way I'm gonna meet a woman who's in the middle of a mess. Me? I want simple, easy, and no drama."

Laughing with the others, Levi said, "I wanted uncomplicated and look what happened to me!"

The welcome party broke up soon after, and he walked with Claire down the lane toward the cabin nestled in the woods near the cliffs. Her eyes were wide as she took in the area.

"This is beautiful, isn't it?" she said, linking fingers with him.

"I thought that the first time I saw it when I came to interview. And I was just thinking that again a little while ago." They reached the door of the cabin and entered an open room, with living room furniture on one side and an open kitchen and dining area on the other. The furniture appeared old but clean and comfortable. An overstuffed, dark green sofa and two chairs, along with a coffee table and a few lamps, all facing the stone fireplace, filled the living room. A small, flat-screen TV placed on a wooden table sat in the corner.

The L-shaped kitchen opened to the space without a counter to divide it. The table was covered with a checkered tablecloth and surrounded by four chairs, their padded cushions matching.

Levi led her toward the back where there was a half bathroom that was wide enough to include a stackable washer and dryer. A large storage closet was across from that room and she spied the back door leading to the yard toward the woods near the cliffs. Opening another door, they discovered a bedroom furnished with a double bed, dresser, and a small closet. Another door led to the attached full bathroom. Walking to the window, she looked out, seeing a view of the rocky shore and water beyond.

"So, what happens next?" she asked, her voice soft as she continued to stare out the window.

"LSI has sent all the records to a contact I have at the Chicago FBI office. They've already been reviewed, and they're going after Mark Martins. The money that had been transferred into your account is now out and in an account that's safe from your boss and officially with the Bureau. My FBI contact will fly out at the end of the week to interview you. Depending on how things go with the case, you might not even have to testify."

Eyes wide, she sucked in a quick breath. "Oh, that would be wonderful!"

"So, you can stay here as you figure out what you want to do."

Her gaze jerked about the room before moving back to his face. She pulled in her lips but remained quiet, her thoughts hidden.

Uncertainty moved over him, and he added, "Upstairs are two more small bedrooms and a bathroom. I was going to offer you this one downstairs, and I'll stay up there."

Her chin lifted as her head jerked back, a crease marring her brow. "Upstairs? I thought… well… um… okay. Yeah… no… I'll take the upstairs bedroom."

He stepped close and reached out his hand to cup her jaw, his thumb sweeping over her cheek. He hated to see the hurt pass through her eyes but didn't want to make any assumptions. "I don't want to fuck this up, Claire. You know I want you. Things have been crazy ever since we met, and I want you to have the time and the space to make decisions that are right for you."

Her gaze never left his as she turned and stepped closer so that their fronts were barely touching. She closed her eyes and leaned slightly into his palm, her breath coming in little puffs. Opening her eyes, she said, "I feel the same about you. I want to be with you, but I don't want to crowd you. This is your space. Your new job. Your new life. I'm just grateful that you've given me a place to stay."

He lifted his other hand and glided his fingers

through her hair, cupping the back of her head. Bending low until their noses almost touched, he breathed her in. As strange as their meeting had been, he could not deny that Claire was the most interesting woman he'd ever met. He had never believed in fate but now wondered if their paths had crossed for reasons far beyond his chance to be a knight in shining armor. "What would you say if I told you I was falling for you? Impetuous? Unrealistic?"

Her lips curved slowly, and she lifted her hands to his waist, her fingertips digging in slightly. "I think I began to fall for you the moment you walked toward me on the side of the road."

A chuckle erupted deep in his chest. "When you looked up at me standing next to your car, I was struck. Didn't have a clue what I was struck with, but I knew something was happening." He lifted his gaze and looked around the bedroom before closing the space between them. "What I didn't know was right then, at that moment, was the beginning of you and me."

Her smile widened, and she said, "So, Levi Amory. Are you asking me to share this room with you?"

He wrapped his arms tighter around her. "Hell yeah, Claire. Share this room, share my life. Let's see where this back road takes us."

Her head fell back so she could hold his gaze. He lifted one hand and skimmed his fingertips over the soft skin of her neck and shoulder, bending to place a light kiss on the pulse point. "You're more beautiful to me right now than anyone I've ever seen."

The smile she gifted him with beamed straight through him. With her still in his arms, their lips met and tongues tangled. Her legs wrapped around his waist and he felt her heat pressing against his swollen cock. Walking the few steps to the other side of the room, he stopped at the bed and gently set her on the edge.

Quickly divesting their clothes, she leaned back and propped her torso up on her elbows. Crawling onto the bed over her body, his heavy weight blanketed her, his torso held up with his forearms planted on either side of her. Their bodies aligned perfectly as his eager cock nudged against her sex and he kissed her sweet lips, his tongue gliding past hers. Lifting away again, he held her gaze. "Whatever this is, Claire, it's not just sex. It's the start of our new adventure. It's the start of us."

One Month Later

Levi glanced over toward Claire in the driver's seat of her new, small SUV. He insisted she purchase something that would be able to handle the Maine winters, and now that she drove to work, she loved it.

She managed to drive, tap her fingers on the steering wheel to the beat of the jazz music on the sound system, and talk all at the same time.

"I really like the Dean of Business," she said. "He

thinks my personal perspective will offer some insight to the class." After her interview with the FBI concerning her findings at Martins & Lee Investment Company, she was able to plan her own future and found another investor position at a female-owned company in a nearby town. She also taught a class in Business Ethics at the local community college one night a week.

Levi had started with LSI, finding the camaraderie to be exactly what he was looking for as well as the stimulation of their missions.

The only thing they had not settled on was a place to live. They had looked for the past two weeks but none of the houses felt right. Now, Claire was driving them to one she discovered online that had just been listed.

As he stared at her profile, he could see her anxiety. "Babe, you said you came earlier today to check this house out with the real estate agent. So, why so nervous?"

She jerked her head to the side, her lips pressed together. "Because I really want it to be right for you."

"Don't you mean for us?"

"Yes, of course, but honestly, Levi… anywhere with you would be perfect for me. But, when I saw this one, I couldn't wait to show it to you. I want it to be just what you'd like to live in."

He tilted his head at her cryptic words and was about to ask more when they turned by a field that was surrounded with woods.

"There's a small bay behind the property that leads

to a larger bay and then the ocean. We're actually only about two miles from Tate and Nora's property."

He looked through the windshield as the large, wooden house came into view and his breath left his lungs in a rush. A large barn complete with gambrel rafters on the two-story section rose before him. Where the hayloft would have been, a large picture window looked over the meadow leading to the woods. A single-story section was connected and included a red front door.

"I didn't want to bring you if it sucked or was a dump," she quickly said, turning to face him after parking outside. "But I went in and, oh, Levi, it's a perfect barn for you."

As soon as he alighted from the SUV, she was right there, linking fingers with him. Words left him, but Claire was so excited, it was easy to remain quiet as she opened the door and led them inside.

"The real estate agent is around but said that she wanted us to have a chance to look it over without her interference."

"Claire, I don't know what to say," he managed to choke out as she dragged him inside the open foyer that led to the large family room on the right. The single-story side had the family room with a stone fireplace, an office, a guest bathroom, and doors leading to a wide deck on the back. The bottom floor of the main barn held the kitchen, dining room, and mudroom with washer and dryer, leading to the double garage. Up the curved wooden stairs were two smaller bedrooms with a full bathroom and the massive master suite, complete with master bathroom and the wide hayloft windows on one wall.

Standing at the window looking over the property, he turned to her, spying the anxious expression on her face. Reaching out, he smoothed the worry line in her brow. "Baby, I don't know what to say. It's amazing. It's more than amazing."

She stepped closer, her front pressed against his, arms around each other's waists, holding each other. Her head tilted back, exposing her soft neck, but it was her dark eyes that held him captive.

"You rescued me and I wanted to give you your heart's desire, Levi."

He bent and kissed her lightly. "Babe, you are my heart's desire."

She smiled, and just like the first time he saw her on the side of the road, it hit him straight through the heart.

"So, what do you think of living in a barn?"

Picking her up, he twirled her around and laughed. "I think living in a barn with you is the perfect continuation of our back road adventure!"

Don't miss the next Lighthouse Security Investigation book.

Click here to order Clay

Lighthouse Security Investigations
Mace

Rank
Walker
Drew
Blake
Tate
Clay

ALSO BY MARYANN JORDAN

Don't miss other Maryann Jordan books!
Lots more Baytown stories to enjoy and more to come!
Baytown Boys (small town, military romantic suspense)
Coming Home
Just One More Chance
Clues of the Heart
Finding Peace
Picking Up the Pieces
Sunset Flames
Waiting for Sunrise
Hear My Heart
Guarding Your Heart
Sweet Rose
Our Time
Count On Me

For all of Miss Ethel's boys:
Heroes at Heart (Military Romance)
Zander
Rafe
Cael
Jaxon
Jayden

Asher

Zeke

Cas

Lighthouse Security Investigations

Mace

Rank

Walker

Drew

Blake

Tate

Hope City (romantic suspense series co-developed with Kris Michaels

Hope City Duet (Brock / Sean)

Carter

Brody by Kris Michaels

Kyle

Ryker by Kris Michaels

Saints Protection & Investigations

(an elite group, assigned to the cases no one else wants…or can solve)

Serial Love

Healing Love

Revealing Love

Seeing Love

Honor Love

Sacrifice Love

Protecting Love

Remember Love

Discover Love

Surviving Love

Celebrating Love

Follow the exciting spin-off series:

Alvarez Security (military romantic suspense)

Gabe

Tony

Vinny

Jobe

SEALs

Thin Ice (Sleeper SEAL)

SEAL Together (Silver SEAL)

Letters From Home (military romance)

Class of Love

Freedom of Love

Bond of Love

The Love's Series (detectives)

Love's Taming

Love's Tempting

Love's Trusting

The Fairfield Series (small town detectives)

Emma's Home

Laurie's Time

Carol's Image

Fireworks Over Fairfield

Please take the time to leave a review of this book. Feel free to contact me, especially if you enjoyed my book. I love to hear from readers!

Facebook

Email

Website

ABOUT THE AUTHOR

I am an avid reader of romance novels, often joking that I cut my teeth on the historical romances. I have been reading and reviewing for years. In 2013, I finally gave into the characters in my head, screaming for their story to be told. From these musings, my first novel, Emma's Home, The Fairfield Series was born.

I was a high school counselor having worked in education for thirty years. I live in Virginia, having also lived in four states and two foreign countries. I have been married to a wonderfully patient man for thirty-five years. When writing, my dog or one of my four cats can generally be found in the same room if not on my lap.

Please take the time to leave a review of this book. Feel free to contact me, especially if you enjoyed my book. I love to hear from readers!

Facebook
Email
Website

Made in the USA
Coppell, TX
08 May 2023